Since the dawn of reading and writing 5,000 years ago, people have looked to books for help in meeting life's perpetual challenges. The problem, of course, is that there are millions of readers so it's nearly impossible for any one book to have answers that every person can use fruitfully. Only a very few texts have ever been able to speak across times, places, and communities to help whomever reads the message. *The Seventh Name of Happiness* is one of those rare, rare books. How does Spero Lappas do it? Well, that's the magic of this marvelous story; a fable for the ages which will reward every individual reader with personal guidance and help in solving life's mysteries. Suffice to say that Dr. Lappas' combination of deep wisdom and empathy make this story special. You need to read it to find out!

Dr. Charles Kupfer
Author of *Something Magic*_and *Indomitable Will*

Advance praise for
The Seventh Name of Happiness

Clio is struggling to succeed in college, to find her place in the world, and most of all, to discover that elusive quality that brings true happiness. Feeling lonely in her new town, she begins to fall into despair, sure that unhappiness has become her lot in life, until she finds she finds the Library on Saga Street and a wise old librarian who assures her that he knows her Perfect Book. With an insightful twist on stories we already know, *The Seventh Name of Happiness* explores our interconnectedness with the world around us and teaches us that, like Clio, we've owned the key to happiness all along. A gem of a read for all ages, and quite likely across the ages, *The Seventh Name of Happiness* offers us not just the beauty of its message, but also the pleasure of the craftsmanship which delivers that message. A lovely gift to rejuvenate our hearts and souls as we find our way through life.

Professor Mary Richards
Associate Professor of English Literature and Composition

The Seventh Name of Happiness

A Fable of Hope and Inspiration

The Seventh Name of Happiness

A Fable of Hope and Inspiration

Spero T. Lappas, PhD

Alithos Media Group, LLC
P.O. Box 6065
Harrisburg, PA 17112

ISBN: 978-0-578-78870-8

Contact the author at Spero@SperoLappas.com

This work is dedicated to
Dr. Thom Lappas,
Alexandria Lappas, Esquire,
Shane Poole, J.D.,
Spero Edward Lappas,
and
Stella Wren Lappas

They are the five names of my happiness.

Prelude

The Fable of the Voyager

A fable is told of a Voyager *who traveled through space and time to discover the secrets of the world and the stars. In every land, he studied the ways of those who knew the names of happiness and sorrow. He preserved their wisdom on parchment and vellum and carried it with him on his journey.*

From time to time he briefly stayed in villages, teaching what he'd learned to those who sought knowledge. The children thought him very old, but to the adults he seemed as young as the ideas he shared. He taught them to love peace, make art, maintain health, and to walk the path of bliss. If he had ever had a name, he never spoke it. He was simply called the Voyager, or the Teacher, or the Wise One.

In time, though, he would leave each place and sojourn anew, seeking new knowledge every moment of every day.

But then, after many years, he wearied of his travels. He stopped at a place beside a stream and a meadow and built himself a house from fieldstone and cedar. At first he was alone, but word spread that a teacher had settled there and visitors would gather every day, sitting on the porch and listen to his lessons. More and more came to the house by the stream and the meadow until the porch was far too small to hold them. So the teacher built a great room in the front of the house and for many months and years he held his lessons there. Other houses rose around him and friendships formed within them. Friendships turned to families, and the families formed a town, all around the Voyager's house of fieldstone and cedar.

The townspeople became farmers, artisans, healers, and merchants. Every evening, after the work of the day had ended, they would come to hear the Voyager read from his parchment and his vellum, and tell them the secrets of the world and the stars.

The Voyager watched the children of that town become parents and the parents grow old and fall, to be buried in a field by the stream and the meadow. In every generation, the children saw him aged and the parents saw him young, but they all knew alike that his lessons brought them happiness and joy.

One evening, when the work of the day had ended, the people came to hear his wisdom; but the Voyager's house was empty. They searched in every room, but he had gone without a trace.

In the great room of the house on a table made of oakwood they found a book covered with blue leather. In its pages were stories of strange and distant places, of times long past and others still to come. After that day, the townspeople would gather in the great room and read the pages of the book and in its words they could hear the wisdom of the Voyager. From that day forward, they lived according to its lessons and they learned the Names of Happiness.

For everyone who read it, it became the Perfect Book.

Part One

The Library on Saga Street

Chapter One

THE LIBRARY ON SAGA STREET

New Year's Day, not so long ago . . .

The Library on Saga Street is always open and always busy on January 1. Everyone makes a New Year's resolution and one of the most popular is "read more good books." That's why we set up special book displays on New Year's Day, right across the lobby from the circulation desk. I call these displays the Resolution Readings and there are mysteries, romances, fantasy, science, and books from every other category. Every year, our *Resolution Books for the Serious Reader* are especially popular. Everyone wants to think of themselves as smart—worthy of picking a book from the "serious" selection. Actually, there's nothing elite about them—we just get suggestions from our librarians and volunteers. But the patrons love them nonetheless and it does get people reading.

The next most popular collection is *Self-Help and Personal Development* and that is not surprising. We all want to improve our lives and become better people. I used to think it was a little sad that people wait for the first page of the calendar to get started on that journey since any day we find our own path of discovery and wonder is a perfect day for new beginnings. If that day happens to be New Year's Day, so be it. That's the day that most folks pick at any rate, and the Resolution Readers think that finding the right book will help them change their lives. Sometimes they are right.

New Year's Day fell on a Monday that year, and the library was crowded with retired people, parents, and young children who were there for Isaac's Story Time (that's me, I'm Isaac) and for our Libraries Rock Book Club. The local schools and college were still on winter break and I was happy to see the library filled with young people. Some joined their little brothers and sisters for story time. Others came to work on their vacation assignments, and some were there to hang out with their friends, filling the tables with giggles and with banter. A few sat in the upholstered armchairs and propped their feet up on the windowsills, wondering about life and all its mysteries. They read a little now and then, but mostly they just looked out the windows at the world thinking of their futures.

Stories. Family. Wonders. Discovery. Those things make libraries magical places and Saga Street is more magical than most. It's been here for a very long time. So have I. In a way, the job I was doing at the library that day was the same job I've done for my entire life.

I looked around the library until I found her, over by the Resolution Readers Book Shelves. She was taller than average, wearing a long tie-dyed skirt and a bright yellow T-shirt. Her auburn hair was pulled back into a ponytail and she wore and round, wire-rimmed glasses. I watched her for about ten minutes while she picked one book after another off the shelf. Each time she would read the cover and then fan the pages with her thumb. She would stop and read a few lines. Then she'd close the book, put it back, and start all over again.

I pushed my reading glasses up on top of my head and strolled across the lobby, stopping about three feet away from her. I put my hands in my pockets and waited for her to notice me. After she rejected her latest possibility, she looked up and said, "Oh."

"Hello," I said. "I don't believe I've seen you here before."

"No." Her voice was soft, almost inaudible. She gave me a wan smile. "I was looking for a book. I was hoping that . . ." But the word for hope died in her throat.

"I really should go home now," she said as she took a step away from the shelves.

"Not everyone has the same hope, but everyone does have a Perfect Book." I ran my fingers across one of the rows of spines and picked one off the shelf. *The Story of Confucius*. "Take this one, for example." She recognized it as one that she had picked up and replaced. "This book has inspired generations of readers. But it's not the Perfect Book for you, is it?" Before she could say a word, I continued. "No. I agree. Not perfect at all. This is a book of rules for living a good life. You probably know all of them already." I watched her from the corner of my eye as I put Confucius back in his slot. "Isn't that so?"

A tiny tear formed in her left eye, behind her glasses. She ignored it and it was gone as quickly as it had appeared. "I don't know anything about life. Everything seems so hard." She looked down at the floor, then back at the bookcase. "I just started college here; my second semester begins next week. But I'm not doing very well." The tear was back again. "I'm smart enough, smarter than other students actually. But I can't concentrate," she was looking straight at me now and talking faster than before. "I'm not happy."

"Ah, happiness! Is that your problem? If so, you are in good company. Some of the smartest men and women in history have tried to understand happiness. What is it? Why is it so important? How do we achieve it? And, most importantly, how do we keep it? You probably believe that success in school will make you happy, but then you tell yourself that you can't have success until after you become happy. It's a vicious cycle that makes you feel worse and worse about your situation, and the whole notion of happiness seems to elude you."

She nodded, not sure what to say. I saw the confusion at the corners of her mouth. She knew that what I said was true, but how did I know so much about her after exchanging so few words?

"Oh, I'm not a mind reader," I assured her. "Not exactly, anyway. We all tend to think that our experiences and problems are brand new in the history of humanity. No one else could have ever felt as awful as we feel right now, could they? Actually, people have struggled to be happy for as long as there have been people, and some of them have learned a few things along the way. Some have even written down the things that they have learned."

I looked to my left and then to my right and stepped a little closer to her. In my best conspiratorial voice, I whispered, "Would you like to read a book? A book that will bring you the happiness you're looking for? Your very own Perfect Book?"

She nodded her head quickly. “Yes. Which one?” she asked, looking at the shelves around her.

“Oh, none of these,” I answered. “Something from our private collection. Come with me, I can always pick the Perfect Book for everyone.” I stepped behind the circulation desk and opened a door marked *Private.* It led to a grand staircase. I started climbing the stairs and, when I saw that she wasn’t following, I called to her. “Quickly. Story Time begins soon. *Aladdin and the Cave*. I don’t want to miss it.”

She took a deep breath, just one, let it out, and followed me up the stairs.

I stopped and turned to her, holding out my hand. “My name is Mr. Atros, but you can call me Isaac.”

“I’m Clio,” she said and shook my hand.

“I’m pleased that I have finally met you,” I said, as we climbed to the top of the stairs.

Chapter Two

SOPHIE AND DOCTOR HIKMA

Many years ago . . .

Doctor Hikma was a general practitioner in the traditional mold, a cradle-to-grave doctor who heard his patients' first breath as they entered this world and held their hands as they left it. He didn't have office hours. "My patients don't have sick hours," he used to say.

He built himself a mansion on Saga Street and put his medical clinic right up front. Any hour of the day the doctor's waiting room was likely to be crowded with coughing, sneezing, hurting, wounded neighbors, none of whom had an appointment. None of them would leave before the doctor saw them, helped them, fixed them up, and, most of all, made them feel important and appreciated. He never spoke about his life before Saga Street and nobody ever asked him. The people were just glad that he had picked their town in which to settle down.

The only time his office was actually closed was in the morning between eight and nine when he went to

Sophie's Café and sat at the table by the window, the big one in the back that looked out upon the stream and the meadow and, beyond that, to the graveyard.

Doctor Hikma walked into Sophie's every morning at eight o'clock sharp and the other customers knew better than to bother him with their aches and pains. This was his private time, and if anyone forgot that, Sophie would chase them away with a few choice words or a whack of her wooden spoon. The doctor always carried a book and Sophie served his breakfast: strong, black coffee and a few slices of sourdough toast. Then she returned to her counter and watched him read. Most days he would absent-mindedly take his blue fountain pen from his jacket pocket, uncap it, and draw a few lines or words in the margin, reminders to his future self of what he had thought about the page the first time he read it. Then, at nine o'clock, Doctor Hikma would walk to his office where another day of worry and reassurance awaited him.

But one day, eight o'clock arrived and Doctor Hikma didn't arrive with it. Maybe he was sick, thought Sophie. Or hurt. Except he never got sick and he never got hurt. None of her other customers knew where he was. She imagined one harmless explanation after another—visiting friends, an emergency out of town, a wedding—

but she didn't believe any of them. When the doctor's table was still empty the next day, and then the day after that, Sophie started to think dark thoughts as she looked out through the window past the meadow. The graveyard made her tremble.

For the next week, Sophie brewed her coffee, baked her bread, and served her customers like nothing was wrong. But then, on a blustery autumn day, she closed up early and headed up to Saga Street and to Doctor Hikma's mansion.

Everything looked normal when she got there, so normal that she almost expected to see the doctor stroll up the side path and tease her for closing the café early. *It must be nice not to have to work for a living,* he would say. But there was no familiar voice, no familiar footsteps. Sophie took a breath and climbed the porch steps to the wide oak doors. She raised her hand to knock but before her knuckles touched the wood the doors swung open as if blown by the wind, but the air was calm around her. She took a deep breath and stepped inside.

The foyer led to the mansion's central room: the library. Scores of walnut shelves were stacked with books on every subject under the sun; they had been shipped here in wooden crates after the house was built. A black lacquered table sat on an Arabian carpet in the center of the room. Statues and busts stood on plaster pedestals. Shakespeare. Moses. Beethoven. Plato. Sophie opened the drapes to admit the afternoon sun. There must have been ten thousand books in that room, and all of them—she remembered fondly—would have a few of the doctor's notes and markings.

She walked through the house and was struck by how normal everything seemed. Everything was neat and tidy. There were no unopened envelopes under the mail slot. No dirty dishes in the kitchen. There wasn't even any dust. She climbed the grand staircase to the second floor and found the beds neatly made and the pillows fluffed. The dresser drawers and closets were filled with clean and folded clothes. If the doctor had disappeared on purpose, she thought, he must have left here naked. The idea made her smile, but then it scared her.

She walked back downstairs and entered the clinic and consulting area. The rolltop desk, with its piles of writing pads and paper, was just as it should have been. Nothing was out of place. She went back into the library and sat in Doctor Hikma's reading chair to rest before walking home. She didn't really know what she had expected to find here, but she certainly hadn't found it. Everything was the same. Everything was perfect.

And then she saw it. On the side table by the chair was a large sealed envelope. At first she thought it must have been a letter that the doctor hadn't gotten around to reading. Maybe it was a patient's medical records sent from out of town. Maybe . . .

As those thoughts flew around in her head, she saw her friend's blue fountain pen lying on top of the envelope.

A few words were written on the outside of the envelope. She recognized Doctor Hikma's handwriting.

Sophie. Read This.

And so she did.

Chapter Three

CLIO IN THE UPSTAIRS ROOM

New Year's Day . . .

"But you can call me Isaac," he said.

Clio knew that she would never call him by his first name. He was old enough to be her grandfather. He had thick white hair, a closely trimmed beard flecked with gray and green eyes with crows-feet from years of hearty smiles. He wasn't tall, he was actually an inch or two shorter than she was, and his old tweed jacket and worn corduroy pants reminded her of her college professors.

It was as if his whole appearance was designed to put people at ease, to encourage them to trust him. To encourage *her* to trust him.

She had come to the Library on Saga Street because of an article in the local newspaper that described the special collections for New Year's Day readers. She wasn't sure if a book could actually help her, but she was willing to give Mr. Atros a chance. After all, he did seem pretty confident. "I always know the Perfect Book for everyone." Why not let him try?

He had already been right about one thing, that much was certain. She was unhappy and she didn't see a way out of it.

She had chosen this college because her excellent high school grades earned her a full scholarship. Her guidance counselor told her that this was one of the best schools in the country, so here she was. But she was sad and lonely almost right away. It was so far from home; she missed her family, her room, everything about her old life. She wanted to drop out and move back to be with her friends, but she knew that wouldn't work. Her friends had all graduated at the same time she did, and they had scattered all over the country—college, jobs, service, you name it.

Clio continued to follow Mr. Atros up the stairs. Was there really a book that could tell you why everything changes and makes you sad? Would that really be her Perfect Book?

"I'm Clio," she said as she shook his hand.

Soon they stood before an ornate pair of double doors next to which there was a bronze plaque that said *Private Room. The Hikma Collection.* Mr. Atros unlocked the doors with a big brass key.

Chapter Four

MR. ATROS AND *THE SEVEN NAMES OF HAPPINESS*

Clio and I sat down in the leather chairs at the black wooden table which was set on the Arabian carpet. She had never heard the story about how the Hikma Mansion became the Library on Saga Street, and as I told it to her she hung on every word. Especially when I got to the part about the Read Me Envelope.

"The envelope contained a letter addressed specifically to her. There was also a key to the mansion and a deed, properly signed, sealed, and totally legal. It was dated on the last day that Doctor Hikma had been in Sophie's café. The deed transferred ownership of the mansion and all its contents to Sophie on the condition that she use the house to start a public library. Sophie took the deed to the next town council meeting and presented it to the mayor. The council was shocked, of course, but everyone agreed that Saga Street would be the perfect place for a library and that the doctor's personal collection would get it off to a fine start.

"News of the envelope that Doctor Hikma had left for Sophie spread throughout the state. Donations to support the Hikma Library began to pour in from all over. Families of the babies he had delivered over the years. The mothers and fathers of sick children whose bedsides he had refused to leave throughout long, dark nights of worry. The high school athletes, now successful adults, whose broken bones and broken hearts he had treated on the sidelines of their dreams. It seemed that everyone had a memory of the doctor's kindness and his wisdom."

I told her how a team of carpenters worked for months to remodel the mansion, dividing some rooms and combining others, until the first floor became one huge open space filled with bookshelves and reading tables. "The grand staircase we just climbed was sealed off behind the circulation desk and the rooms on the second floor became offices and meeting spaces. This room now holds a special collection chosen from Doctor Hickma's original books. Each volume in this room was carefully selected by Sophie who said that these were the ones which most clearly expressed the doctor's personal philosophy. There are about a hundred books here. They are all are stacked on the bookshelves around you. Except for that one." I pointed off into a corner at a locked glass case set upon a small round table. Then, I turned back to Clio and finished my story.

I told her how the governor had attended the library's dedication because Doctor Hikma had once saved his wife from influenza. The mayor gave a speech about how much Doctor Hikma had meant to the community and he teared up a little when he said that even though this library was wonderful for the town he would much rather have the doctor back here, listening to the stories of his patients' aches and pains. In spite of all the dignitaries and celebrities in attendance, the ribbon-cutting honors belonged to Sophie who said a few words about the table by the window, and the meadow and the stream, and then promised that in this library everybody would always be allowed to write in the books, just as Doctor Hikma had. She opened the doors with the big brass key and then walked back to her café to take care of her lunch customers.

"I want to show you something very special." I walked to the locked glass case. "This was the first book that Sophie picked to go into this room."

I took a key from my pocket, unlocked the case, and removed a book bound in blue leather. The cover was worn with age and the spine was cracked. "You'll have to be careful. It's very old." I carried it to the table where Clio sat.

"A great many people have read this book over many, many years. Some say that it has changed their lives."

I placed the book on the table and opened it to the title page.

"It's called *The Seven Names of Happiness* and I have always known that for you, today, this would be the Perfect Book."

"Always known?" She was confused. "How could you have . . ."

I smiled as I walked away from the table. "Don't fret about that," I said. "Just remember that the library closes at six o'clock."

But she didn't hear me. She was already engrossed in the first chapter by the time I reached the door.

Part Two

The Names of Happiness

The Seven Names of Happiness

Introduction to The Voyager's Tale

I have been known by many names in many places. *For those of you who read these words, you may think of me as The Voyager, as one who has journeyed far and wide through space and time to learn the secrets of the world and the stars. In every land to which I traveled, I studied the ways of men and women who knew the names of happiness and sorrow.*

I journeyed first to the east of the Great Ocean and to the Land Beside the Sky. There I would meet the Dragon Prince and learn the First Name of Happiness.

The First Name of Happiness

The Story of the Dragon Prince

***For many years** the Dragon King ruled the Land Beside the Sky, keeping his people safe in fragile peace with armies, laws, and conquests. He felt that peace and safety would make his people happy, for their happiness was his object and his goal.*

But then one day, as all men do, the Dragon King grew old and died and was buried in the mountains according to the rites of his tradition. His son, a man of youth and conscience, prepared to take the throne. He wondered if his father's ways were truly best for his subjects, if laws and powers were the surest path to happiness. So he studied with the sages and the shamans of his kingdom and they told him of the knowledge they had gathered. Philosophers and scientists knew many things about happiness and the prince sought to learn them all.

The lessons that he learned made the Dragon Prince the wisest of all rulers.

I followed the old Silk Road and the trade routes to the top of the highest mountains. One morning, I awoke in my campsite to the music of human voices raised in song, drifting through the valleys. I folded my sleeping rugs and followed the sound to a clearing bathed in sunlight and bright colors. Half marketplace, half carnival, it was filled with traders and magicians, singers, cooks, and sellers; tapestries and drummers and merchants with their produce. Children danced throughout the streets in capes of red and purple while their parents watched and smiled in pride and gladness. Older men and women sat with tea and conversation. I knew that I had found the Dragon Kingdom, but this was not a land of armies or of weapons. Instead, it was a land of jubilation.

I watched the celebration as I walked amidst the crowd. I found a tiny inn whose open doors welcomed me to enter. Inside was the innkeeper, her dress was as yellow as the sun and her long braided hair was the color of starlight.

"You have picked the perfect day to visit us, dear stranger" she said. "Tonight, the people will

meet in the Great Hall and assemble for The Making of Decisions."

"The Making of Decisions? What is that?" I asked. But instead of an answer, she took my canvas bag, placed it on the floor, and led me to a table by her fire.

"First, you rest and eat. Only then will I answer your questions." She brought me bowls of dates and lentils, a pie of leeks and raisins, bread, and tea and honey. "We welcome every traveler to our land. Many are the ones who come to hear the Dragon Prince, to learn the Name of Happiness.

I ate till I was full and my hostess pulled a chair up to my table. She took the last date from the earthen bowl that she had placed before me. We spoke until the sun set and then she led me through the main street of the village to a building made of stone with iron doors. Scores of other villagers walked with us and all entered, seating themselves on benches and floor cushions. The hall was lit with candles and lanterns all around the outer walls; in the center was an open space where no one walked or sat. Three fireplaces, each one large enough for a person to walk upright inside it, blazed with piled logs. The room was warm and bright despite the winter wind outside.

Within moments, all conversation ceased and the crowd grew silent. A young man, no older than I, entered and stood in the open space. His face was smooth and unworried and he wore long robes as green as summer leaves. "Here is the Dragon Prince," my companion told me. "Now he will tell the Parable."

The Dragon Prince took a scroll from within the folds of his robe. He opened it and read.

"A hundred years ago, perhaps a thousand, an aged monk set out on foot to reach his monastery, high atop the Great Mountain. The trek was long and dangerous, and the monk grew weary and tired. Eventually he could walk no farther. He spread his prayer rug on the snow and settled down to await the transition that comes to every man.

"Three brothers were hiking through the mountains and came upon the monk. They wrapped him in their blankets and built a fire to warm him. They gave him food from their packs and tea made with melted snow.

"When the monk was strong enough to travel, the brothers built a litter out of branches and woolen blankets. They placed him on top and took turns carrying him through the mountain paths and passes.

He gave them directions to his monastery and they reached it on the third day of their travels.

"At the monastery, the other monks and the abbot greeted them warmly and with gratitude. When their friend had failed to arrive as expected, they had feared the worst. Now their minds were at ease. The three brothers looked around in amazement at the beauty of the place the monks had built for themselves atop the Great Mountain. They had long heard tales of the Diamond Monastery, a place of truth and magic, but they doubted them and had thought them all the stuff of legends and of myth. But now, they saw the monastery for themselves and they remembered that the stories taught that this was a place where miracles could happen.

"The Abbot knew their thoughts and nodded kindly. 'What has been your rescue of our colleague from the cold if not a miracle of kindness? In gratitude, I offer you another. It is within my power in this place to grant you each one wish to thank you for his life. Think wisely and choose well, for once your wish is spoken it will come to be a fact and can never be recalled. Take care to pick the thing most sure to make you happy.'

"The oldest brother spoke first. 'I have always wished that I had been born a king, the ruler of a mighty empire. Kings have wealth and power and those who sit upon a throne, being born to grace and royalty, must certainly be happy. Their nature and heredity assure it. And so, kind abbot, if such a thing may be within your power, I wish for you to change my history and birthright that I may be a king.'

"The middle brother spoke next. 'I wish for luck and fortune,' he said. 'With favor and good fortune all wondrous things inevitably will follow. Riches. Opportunity. Fame and favored status. I will be wealthy and admired and will buy whatever else I wish to have, my heart's every desire. I have no doubt that certainly I will then be glad and happy.'

"The abbot listened patiently. When the first two brothers had finished speaking, he closed his eyes and raised his hand before them. Opening his eyes again he said, 'It is now just as you wish. When you return home the things that you have spoken will be true. Royal birth. Power. Wealth. Fame. Good fortune. All of that awaits you. May you always think that you have chosen wisely.'

"The two older brothers shouted with joy and it did seem to everyone assembled that they were, if only for the moment, truly happy.

"But then the abbot turned to the youngest brother. 'And you,' he asked. 'What is your one wish, the one which must come true?'

"The youngest brother spoke. 'It seems to me quite clear that if it is happiness I seek then that should be my wish and simply that. Will power make me happy? Or royal birth? Or wealth? Maybe. Maybe not. No one sees the future. No one knows. But happiness alone is always sought as the greatest of good things, so it makes the most sense to seek it for itself. Why should I wish for other things in the uncertain hope that they may lead to happiness? No. I will instead choose happiness by its own name. That is my wish, wise monk, if you have the power here to grant it. I wish for you to teach me to be happy.'

"The two older brothers left the mountains and went back to their homes where they found everything exactly as they had wished. The youngest of the three stayed behind within the Diamond Monastery. He studied with the abbot, learning many powerful lessons. When he finally returned to his home he found his brothers there with their power,

wealth, and fortune. But it was he, the wise young brother, who for a long and joyful life was known to all the people as the happiest man alive."

The Dragon Prince stopped reading and put away the scroll. "And so, dear friends, having heard again The Parable of the Three Brothers, we come together in assembly to make wise choices and decide how best to maintain happiness."

The prince and all his people stayed assembled through the night and spoke of how to rule a happy kingdom. They made decisions about how to educate their children, about how to help the elderly and the sick, the hurt and the lame. How best to care for the space within which they all lived, and how to resolve disputes when they arose. Each choice was based on what would make the people happy rather than rich, renowned, or powerful. Each time they reached consensus, the prince would unwrap the Scroll of the Parable and record the decision. At the first light of morning, the meeting ended and the people went to their homes to rest and be renewed in the knowledge that a happy day awaited.

Only the Dragon Prince and I remained in the Great Hall. He came to where I was and sat beside me. "I heard that there was a visitor in our midst, a Voyager from afar. The people of this kingdom have heard the Parable of the Three Brothers many times and they understand it. But since you have come here seeking knowledge, I will tell you what it means.

"We call it a parable because it teaches a universal truth in the form of a story. Its universal truth is this: just as there are three brothers in the story, the teachers of all ages have shown that human happiness is a substance composed of three elements.

"First, our individual nature—which we often tend to overlook. Just as nature makes some people taller and others shorter, some strong and others weaker, our heredity and birthright predisposes some to become happier than others. This may seem unfair, but fair or not it is the law of nature. For some, bliss and contentment come easier than to others. The first brother counted on nature and heredity to bring him happiness, so he wished to be a king. But as powerful as heredity may be, it is just one third of happiness, and it does not rule our lives.

"Next, our circumstances and station in life play a role. Wealth creates happiness more surely than does poverty, and health more surely than does sickness. But we overestimate the role of circumstance

and so we tend to purchase it as a substitute for happiness. This is the lesson of the middle brother, who thought that luck and fortune would suffice to make him happy.

"But who has not seen a happy beggar or a blissful invalid and do we not also know miserable tycoons and doleful athletes? The person who seeks wealth or power or station because they assume happiness will follow makes the same error as the two older brothers of the parable: In seeking happiness by its proxies they mistook the path for the destination. The teachers with whom I have studied know that no one wise would choose tormented power, sorrowful wealth, or painful fame and status over the simple happiness which flourishes from a well-lived life.

"What the lessons of the ages teach is that happiness, unlike wealth or power, or even health or strength, is the single human condition that is treasured for its own true self. The parable reminds us that men and women err when they try to bring about happiness indirectly, wishing for wealth and fine possessions or for status or for fame. These may be enjoyed by some, but in truth they are never valued on their own account. Instead, people value them for that which they might bring. Joy, contentment, happiness. Here is the lesson

of the parable: No one wishes to be happy in order to then have something better. Happiness, and happiness alone, is valued for itself. The youngest brother knew that and so he chose it in its own authentic name."

"But why then did he stay behind when his brothers returned home?" I asked. "If the abbot granted his wish for happiness, what more was there to learn?"

"Alas, dear Voyager, you do not yet understand the parable. The true Names of Happiness do not arise automatically like nature or circumstance. Rather, they reside within our choices and behaviors. That is what we study at the Council of Decisions.

"We gather in assembly to make the wisest choices and to choose directions and behaviors that will produce the greatest happiness. That is my responsibility as prince, but it is also the responsibility of every living soul.

"As men and women, we cannot change our hereditary nature as the oldest brother sought to do. As humans we are born with human foibles, with the limits of our species. We must accept that as a fact, but not the only fact, of life.

"As for luck and fortune, we live with good and bad alike. The middle brother wished for perfect circumstances, but here in the Dragon Kingdom we

have learned that we cannot flatten the mountains to make them easier to climb. The snow will come in winter and the cold will chill our bones, no matter what fair weather we desire.

"But with wisdom we can learn to make good choices and with wisdom we can decide how best to overcome the limitations of our nature and to adjust to our surroundings. Therefore, all around you see a land of happiness."

The prince continued his lesson. "Every person is a kingdom unto themselves. Just as our kingdom makes laws for the good of its people, every person must make laws to govern their time on Earth. These laws are the choices we make about how we shall live our lives for happiness and meaning. Just as it is the obligation of a prince to make his people happy, so it must be the obligation of the individual to make a happy life and to do so deliberately, consciously, and with intention. Happiness is nothing less than the essential duty of our existence.

"There are many Names of Happiness, friend Voyager, but its first Name is Responsibility. It is our responsibility to live a complete life and not to squander our essence on woe and gloom and worry. We in the Dragon Kingdom could choose to curse the

snow and the harshness of the cold. Instead, we choose to celebrate the beauty of the vistas and the comfort of the hearth. We live within our nature and our circumstance, but they do not control us. It is our gift, and our burden, to be free."

As the Dragon Prince spoke those words to me, I followed his meaning. "We must be the rulers of our character, the legislatures of our disposition. By the inner council of our wisdom we create a happy life."

The prince's smile told me that I understood him, but I had still one more question. "You have said that the responsibility to choose wisely is the First Name of Happiness. But how does one choose wisely?"

"Those were the lessons that the youngest brother stayed behind to learn, but I am not the Abbot of the Diamond Monastery and I cannot work miracles." The prince rose to bid me farewell. "The other Names of Happiness are spread upon the world, but you must find them for yourself. Tomorrow, when you leave the Dragon Kingdom, you must travel to the City of the Golden King; then to the Valley of the Ancient Battle; and then you must sail on the Moonlight Ship to the Island of the Fisher

King. There is much for you to know."

I was weary from the day and night and I fell asleep right there where I sat. When I awoke the embers in the fireplaces were dim and the Great Hall was empty except for me alone.

I gathered my belongings and struck out on the next leg of my voyage, over land and sea to find the first place the Dragon Prince had named.

"How do you like it so far?" I asked. Clio hadn't noticed when I re-entered the room.

"It's, it's amazing. It's wonderful. But is it . . ."

"True?" I finished her question. "Well, the Land of the Dragon Prince is true. It's a real place called the Kingdom of Bhutan, a land older than the pyramids, where the people design national policies to contribute to their happiness. Other countries measure wealth or their gross national product, but Bhutan observes a National Happiness Index. Other countries make decisions that will make them powerful or rich, but the Bhutanese people make decisions about public life that they expect will make them happy."

Clio had never heard about the Kingdom of Bhutan or the National Happiness Index and she listened intently. "As for the Parable of the Three Brothers, that may be a story, no one knows if it's true or not. But the lesson of the parable, the three elements of a happy life, is a scientific truth. It is a psychological fact that happiness results from the combination of heredity, circumstance, and personal behavior."

I pulled out a chair and sat down. I took a piece of paper and my pen from my pocket and drew a circle divided into three unequal sections. "First, you have to understand the concept of your *happiness potential.*

That's where the three elements come into play." I filled in one section of the circle with my pen. "About half of our happiness potential comes from heredity. Some people get a genetic head-start—they're born with a greater tendency to be happy. It just comes naturally to them. You probably know some of these people. Maybe you are one."

"Hardly," she whispered.

I smiled at her. "No matter what happens—misery, misfortune, or loss—they can stay cheerful. For others, it's not so easy. Just as the Dragon Prince couldn't change human nature, none of us can change our genetic happiness potential.

"Another ten percent is determined by major life conditions." I filled in a smaller section of the circle. "Think of the mountains and the cold in the Dragon Kingdom. Here again, luck plays a role in human affairs and scientists have confirmed what you have probably always suspected: Our potential for happiness suffers from the vagaries of chance.

"The mistake that many people make is that they believe that these two elements are the whole circle. It's easy for some people to let themselves off the hook and accept a mediocre existence by submitting to the misfortunes of nature and circumstances. Bad genes, bad luck—that's it, right? Not at all.

"After those first two elements, we still have all of this." I pointed to the large, unfilled, section of the circle. "That leaves forty percent which we can control for ourselves, and the good news is that this is enough all by itself to create a high level of happiness. This is where our intentional choices and behaviors have been scientifically proven to produce happiness. If we identify and practice the most beneficial behaviors, then we will make ourselves happier. It's as simple—and as difficult—as that."

Clio wondered aloud, "Do you really believe that?"

I smiled. "Of course I believe it. But it wouldn't matter if I believed it or not. It's a scientific truth, a universal law, like gravity or motion. Many years ago, long before the scientists confirmed this, Abraham Lincoln said that people are just about as happy as they make up their minds to be. And another wise man, I think his name was Emerson, said that the only person you are destined to be is the one you decide to be. They were really on to something, don't you agree?"

I pointed at the piece of paper again. "This knowledge is very empowering once we understand that anyone can be happy no matter what their heredity and circumstances may be. Look at it this way: Some people may have a head start on happiness, but no one has a head start on *unhappiness*. The Bhutanese people believe that you will feel happy when you choose a path of consequence and beauty. I think they would agree with Lincoln: We can all be as happy as we make up our minds to be.

"The harder question, of course, is this: How do we make up our minds to be happy?"

I could see that Clio was thinking hard. "Have you read this book, Mr. Atros? The whole thing I mean?"

"Yes, my young friend. I read it a very long time ago. *The Seven Names of Happiness* are true. So far you have only read about the first one. Would you like to read the rest? Now that you know that the quest for happiness imposes upon us the responsibility to make wise choices, do you want to learn about those choices?"

She nodded her head with excitement.

"Then keep reading. You can learn the Names of Happiness just as the Voyager learned them.

I headed for the door. "Just remember, we close at six o'clock tonight."

"Mr. Atros?" I stopped and turned around.

"Was the Voyager a real person? Or is all of this just a fairy tale?"

"*Just* a fairy tale?" I repeated. "Let's see now.

How do fairy tales usually begin? *Once upon a time*, right? Well, once upon a time the Voyager was flesh and blood and as real as you or me. Maybe he still is."

I left her with the book and she quickly turned the page.

The Next Name of Happiness

The Story of the Golden King

I traveled west, *following ancient roads to Asia Minor until I reached a desert plain surrounded by dense forests to the north and to the west. It was an area of farmers and herdsmen which the people there called Phrygia, in the land of Anatolia.*

The people of Phrygia had once fought with the Trojans against the mighty Greeks, resisting and withstanding a siege of many years until the Trojan Horse deceived them and betrayed them. Now they lived in peace, practicing trades and artistry. Every part of the venerable city was adorned with paintings and murals and other decorations. As I wandered through the streets, I found the greatest masterpiece of all in the sun-drenched central courtyard. A statue made of gold.

It was mounted high above me on a triangular pedestal of stone. As tall as a man and perfectly formed, he wore a regal crown and the garments of a king: flowing robes and sashes and a cape that reached his feet. His head was tilted backwards and his right hand held his brow. He wore a countenance of misery unbridled, a frozen scream of agony and pain. Three sides of the pedestal held plaques of shining brass.

The court was filled with benches made of wood and iron nails, so I sat myself upon one and studied the gold figure cast before me. What awful happenstance or injury had painted such a face of pure unhappiness and woe?

Just then, a father led his son into the courtyard.

"Behold, my son," the father spoke. "The lesson of the tortured Golden King whose choices brought him pain and forever crushed his gladness."

He placed his spectacles upon his face and turning to the first plaque read aloud.

"Before you stands King Midas, the wealthiest man alive. I ruled the land of Phrygia from the forest to the sea.

"My father was King Gordius known

throughout the land for craft and earthly wile. My mother was a child of mighty Zeus. Fate and birth had graced me with every kind of blessing. Family and friends. Power and good fortune. The greatest was my daughter, so beautiful and pure that I named her after life itself: Zoe, in the language of my people.

"But in spite of every blessing, I was more greedy and dissatisfied than any man alive. Each day when I awoke, I wished to have more gold than other men. Consumed by that ambition, I longed, indeed, to have the Golden Touch of legend so that everything I touched would turn to gold.

"Eventually, the universe agreed and I became the man whose merest touch turned everything to gold. Rejoicing in that power, I held the humblest bricks and they became gold ingots. The stones and rocks as well became gold nuggets in my hand.

"My servants followed me as I raced throughout the kingdom, transforming every common thing into a treasure of great worth. They gathered them behind me and laid them in a warehouse by my palace. Day after day I built ever greater stores of gold, never sleeping, never eating, simply adding to my treasures and my wealth. I thought that I had chosen well and wisely and that now, at last, my

happiness was proved.

"In time, though, I grew hungry and, returning to my palace, I entered the dining hall and sat at my table. Days had passed since my last meal and my cooks produced a splendid banquet to satisfy my appetite. I took my knife and fork, and each one, at my touch, turned to gold. I marveled at the glistening utensils and wondered with a smile if there could be a limit to my wealth.

"But when I cut a piece of meat and placed it in my mouth it was meat no longer. The touch of my lips and tongue turned it into solid gold. No longer food, I spit it out upon the floor lest I should choke and die. I knew at once my peril and mistake. No longer could I eat or even drink, for everything my body touched would be transformed to gold. Inedible and poisonous, every morsel would destroy me.

"'Oh, Universe,' I cried. 'My dearest wish has been achieved. Must I now die of hunger?' My servants watched in terror and dismay as I stood up in confusion. They shrank away from me and ran, fearing I would touch them and they would be transformed.

"I sat back down, exhausted, not knowing what to do. I feared that I would perish from starvation and thirst, alone and feared and shunned by all around me,

the loneliest, most pitiful of men, my wealth of no importance.

"Those thoughts ran through my mind as my beloved daughter Zoe dashed into the dining hall. She had missed me in the days that I had wandered through the countryside testing my new power and, crying 'Father! Father! You are home with me at last!' she leaped into my lap.

"Before I could avoid her kiss upon my cheek, her lips touched my face. And, in touching me, her flesh became as hard as metal; her body now a golden statue, cold and heavy, she toppled to the floor.

"I gazed at her in horror and wished a different wish aloud. 'Oh, that this power would be taken from me now and my daughter be restored!'

"As I screamed in desperation with my face a mask of anguish, my right hand flew to my brow as if to hold my suffering in place. And by touching my own self, I became the wretched thing that you now see before you. The golden touch for which I had so long hoped destroyed me in an instant."

The father looked to his son who was listening carefully. He turned to the second plaque and read further. "My name is Princess Zoe, child of Midas,

King of Phrygia, whose tale you now know. His ingratitude once cursed me to a golden form, but my innocence restored me to a life of flesh and blood. Unlike me, my father's greed and thanklessness have condemned him to the fate you see before you: Fixed for all eternity in sadness and in gloom. I have placed him in this courtyard and written his story upon these plaques so that you may learn the lesson of his injudicious craving. Look upon his agony, oh kinsman, neighbor, traveler, and know from his example the dear price of foolish longing."

The father finished reading and returned his spectacles to his pocket. He knelt by his son and placed his arms around him.

When once again the father stood, the child spoke to him and asked, "What was the king's mistake, Father? Is it wrong to hope for riches?"

"No, my child. Riches by themselves contain no evil. The lesson of the plaques comes from a recognition of all that Midas had before his wish was granted. His blessings filled every part of his life. Royal birth and family, a loving daughter, the affection of his neighbors. And yet, he could not appreciate them because his mind always turned to the one thing he did not already have: the Golden

Touch. He squandered the contentment that comes from enjoying every day and every hour. Such was the folly of the Golden King and that is why his daughter placed him here, so that all may see his terror and despair, that we may learn his lesson, and learning it be spared his same undoing."

The father led the son away from the statue and they sat on a bench beside my own. So attentive to each other, they did not notice that I had overheard their conversation.

"You see, my son," the father said, "there are many Names of Happiness and one of the dearest of them all is Gratitude." The child seemed confused so the father continued. "Gratitude, which is within the reach of everyone, gives us the power to ward off sorrow and to guard against dissatisfaction. In gratitude, we are certain to be happy.

"By practicing gratitude we appreciate everything that is valuable and meaningful in our lives—we remain aware and give thanks for the good things life gives us. Unlike the foolish king we do not waste our lives longing after things that are absent or imperfect. Instead, we concentrate on the goodness that surrounds us and hold a grateful wonder. With gratitude, we give thanks for every blessing we might

otherwise take for granted.

"In doing this, we live a life of greater enjoyment and pleasure; we are better friends and kinsmen. Our eyes are bright, our steps are sure, and we live with more compassion.

"In a world so full of riches of the spirit and the heart, it does no good to miss and mourn the things that we may lack. King Midas had a kingdom and a daughter's love. He stands before us now, a tormented, golden wretch. Gratitude, and gratitude alone, would have saved him from his torment. That is the lesson of this place and that is why we come here."

The father placed a kiss on his son's cheek. "Someday you will be the father and your child will look to you for meaning. Return to this place often and read the words of Zoe, whose name itself means life, and allow her wisdom and her lesson to guide you." And then, together, hand in hand, they left the courtyard and headed home.

I approached the Golden King and saw the message of the third plaque. "Be grateful for all the things you have and remember how much you would miss them if they were gone. Do not be like King Midas and ignore the wonders the world puts before you, pining instead for a gift you do not have. Thanksgiving is a golden Name of Happiness."

I gazed again up at the model of perpetual despair and left the Golden King behind, a man whose final lesson came too late to make him happy.

The Next Name of Happiness

The Story of the Valley of Elah

***I stayed for thirteen days** in Phrygia, the City of the Golden King, and on each of those days I returned to the central courtyard where I read again the plaques and meditated on the Legend of the Statue. I studied the worth of gratitude and realized with greater strength each day that happiness is impossible without it.*

Just as we are responsible for the decisions of our lives, so are we bound by reason and decency to be aware of the good things that surround us. The big things, like the daughter's love which King Midas took for granted, but the small ones too. The breathing of the air. The beating of our hearts. The beauty of a flower and the sky. When I believed that I understood the Second Name of Happiness, I packed my canvas bag and headed to the city's main bazaar. There I would seek passage for my eastward voyage to the Valley of the Ancient Battle, the next place named by the Dragon Prince where I would learn a Name of Happiness.

I wandered through the aisles of the bazaar, each one packed with stands and tables piled with tapestries and bronze, spice and fragrant oils. On the afternoon of my second day there, I met a merchant traveler named Stavros. He told me that his wagons would soon depart for the ancient cities of Azekah and Socho where he would sell olives and pistachios and trade for incense, dates, and amber.

"Between those cities is the Valley of Elah which you seek," he told me. "Would you become a merchant on our voyage and travel with the caravan?"

I agreed. For six days I joined with Stavros's workers loading the wagons and filling them with provisions for the long journey ahead of us. We set out on the seventh day and traveled east through the lands of Lycaonia and Cappadocia, where the people made their homes in caves and the land is said to look like the surface of the Moon. Then we turned south and soon the road and trails ended. For days we made slow progress, but Stavros knew the land and all its stories and at every turn and landmark he told me the history of the places and the memories that lived for him in each field, stream, and hill.

After many days of rough travel we reached the plains of Israel and the mountains of the West Bank. Stavros took our wagons through a mountain pass and we were in the field of the terebinths, the stately oaks abundant in that valley.

After the entire caravan had entered the great plain, I bid Stavros to sit with me under a shade tree and tell me all the secrets of that place.

"Why do you suppose that the Dragon Prince sent me here to learn a Name of Happiness?" I asked.

Stavros mussed his white beard and stood to stretch his legs. The travel had been arduous, and soon the work of setting up the trading tents and unloading all the wagons would begin. "I have heard of the wisdom of the Dragon Prince of the Land Beside the Sky," he said. "Was it he who sent you to Anatolia to learn the Story of the Golden King?" He lifted his canteen and took a long drink.

"Yes," I answered. "The Prince sent me there and here as well, and from here to the Island of the

Fisher King. In Phrygia, I learned a lesson from the Legend of the Statue, but what can this place, an empty valley between two mountains, teach me of the Names of Happiness?"

He sat back down beside me. It was cool under that tree with the sun past noon and the grass was soft and lush. "I have traveled many times to this very spot," he said. "For many years, since long before you were born, I have pitched my tents and made my marketplace right here." He glanced at the wagons as his crews had already started raising up the tent poles and the canopies. He smiled and his eyes were moist as he looked beyond them into another age. "Now I must leave that work to younger men and stronger. But a time there was when I could myself unload ten wagons in the time that five young men spend planning their next move."

He laughed at his exaggeration and pointed at the hill to the east.

"Imagine that hillside thick with soldiers, each one covered with armor and carrying a shield and a battle lance. Waiting for the battle cry to sound, they slice slabs from the carcasses of goats and lambs turning on spits over cooking fires. They were the descendants of the Egyptians and the

cousins of Mesopotamia. They were gathered for war against their sworn enemies the Israelites, to whom they were known as the Philistines.

"It was thousands of years ago. The Philistines and the Israelites had gathered here for the final conflict which would decide for once and all time who would rule the lands of Palestine. The Philistines were mighty warriors. They had defeated the Israelites once before at the battle of Eben-Ezer, where they killed thirty thousand men and captured the Ark of the Covenant. Then, right here in this valley, they sought to crush the nation of Israel and enslave all of its people. The Philistines were massed on that hillside. The Israelites waited on the other and they were afraid.

"One day, the Philistines sent their greatest warrior to the edge of the hillside. He was a giant, over nine feet tall. His armor weighed a hundred pounds, his spear was as long as a weaver's rod, and it was headed with a point made of iron. His name was Goliath and he had trained from his youth to be a fighter. His whole life prepared him for that moment.

"When he left the camp of the Philistines, he called out to the Israelites that they should bring him their champion to fight him man-to-man and have the

victor's army deemed the winner of the battle. Every morning and every night for forty days, Goliath shouted the same challenge but none of the men of Israel dared to answer. Instead, they fled from the sight of the giant.

"As the stalemate dragged on day after day, a father named Jesse sent his youngest son to bring food and provisions to his other sons who fought with the army of Israel. The young boy tended his father's sheep and played the harp; he had never been a soldier nor learned the ways of war. But when he came to this valley, he heard Goliath's challenge and he wondered what the king would give to a fighter who could defeat the giant. Great riches would belong to such a fighter, he was told, but his brothers and the other soldiers laughed at his pretension. How could such a boy think that he could slay Goliath? It was ridiculous. The greatest warriors of Israel feared the giant; a simple boy without a sword or armor would never stand a chance.

"Finally, he was taken to the king who asked him how he could dare imagine himself victorious when his finest warriors are afraid. The boy told the king that when he tended his father's sheep, sometimes a wolf or a lion or a bear would steal one away. 'I have

chased the vicious lions and held them by the throat. I have killed the wolves and bears just to save a single sheep. How much more shall I do to save the land of Israel?'

"The king was impressed by the boy's daring and he agreed to let him fight Goliath. He outfitted him with armor and shields and weapons, but those things made the boy uncomfortable so he took them off and left them all behind. Instead, he made for himself a sling on a leather strap and found a smooth stone in a stream bed. The next time Goliath shouted out his challenge to the Israelites the shepherd boy stepped forward. The Philistine laughed and made ready to throw his spear, as long as a weaver's rod with a spearhead made of iron. But before the warrior threw his spear, the boy placed his stone in the pocket of his sling and launched it straight and true. It struck Goliath's forehead and the giant fell to the ground like a great tree felled by the woodsman's axe. With the giant dead, the Israelites were victorious."

Stavros hesitated for a moment as he caught his breath. It was as if he were caught up in the moment of that decisive battle.

"That boy's name was David and the king, true to his promise, gave him great riches. He

became the anointed king of Israel and he has been admired by all generations.

"Now that I have told you the story of this place, young friend, let me ask you a question. Why do we admire David for his courage? Is it because of his victory over Goliath?"

I thought for a moment and then agreed. "Yes, I believe that is true. He was braver than every other soldier. He stepped forward to fight a giant, so he must have been a hero."

"I see," said Stavros, with his mouth twisted in the start of a smile. "If we admire David because of his daring in battle, then what shall we think of Goliath's bravery? He promised to fight any warrior who would face him. For all he knew the Israelites had a giant of their own—perhaps one even bigger, stronger, with a longer spear, better trained. Goliath dared to fight anyone, without exception. David, on the other hand, knew in advance whom he had to fight. If courage is simply bravery in battle, perhaps Goliath demonstrated as much bravery, maybe even more, than David. If he had slain the shepherd boy, would the entire world admire Goliath's achievement and his courage?"

"No. I don't think so. But . . ." I was sure

that David had shown greater courage than Goliath, but I could not find the words to answer Stavros's question.

"No, I do not believe so either," said Stavros with certainty. "Goliath was formidable, but his boldness was more reckless than brave. He rushed headlong into confrontation, he disdained the challenge of David, and he scorned the threat which he presented. In the end, he paid the price with his death, with the defeat of his army, and with the conquest of his people. He was a daredevil, not a hero. No matter how the Battle of Elah might have ended, it would always have been David and not Goliath who would be honored for his courage."

"But the Dragon Prince sent me here to learn one of the Names of Happiness, not to hear a tale of battles. What can David's story teach me about happiness?"

"Courage in the face of physical danger may be praise-worthy," explained Stavros. "But even villains sometimes show that kind of bravery. David's courage was of a different kind. He didn't come here to fight a great battle and liberate his people, he was sent here on the simple mission of delivering food to his brothers. But

when he was confronted with the opportunity and the necessity of saving his people, he showed true courage by involving himself in the passion of the world around him. And he did that," Stavros waved his finger at me for emphasis, *"while still remaining authentic to his true nature."*

"The kind of genuine courage that comes from daring to live a life of integrity is your next Name of Happiness. Do you imagine that only warriors can be brave? Imagine the artist who struggles against the uncertainty of creation to bring forth originality out of nothing. Consider the parent who makes sacrifices large and small to raise a family and nurture children to their greatness. Think of the discouraged explorer or researcher who dares to look beyond disappointment to try again. What about the friend who forgives a harsh betrayal and takes another chance on connection or on love? Those are occasions for courage which men and women can face at any moment and from which they can squeeze the fullness of potential and the richness of destiny. Courage arises as we accept the ordinary realities of life instead of wishing that the world was different than it is. David did not conquer the world by wishing that there was no Goliath, but by daring

to engage with the reality that surrounded him.

"David entered this valley as a shepherd and fought his battle using the experiences he had gathered over a lifetime of guarding sheep. Fighting Goliath with a lance or a spear would not have been right for him, and so the story of David holds a vital lesson for all of us. We can all use the gifts we already possess to become a champion.

"Or a king.

"Or a merchant."

He placed his hand gently upon my shoulder. "Or a Voyager."

Night had fallen and the sky was filled with stars. All of the workers had set their bedrolls under the wagons. Only Stavros and I remained awake.

"The reality of this present moment tells me, young friend, that there will not be many more caravans for me." I started to speak, but Stavros waved me to silence. "No matter. A young man has ambitions and an old man has nostalgia. The accomplishments of which you dream are for me the memories of achievement. My past was once the future which now beckons you with promise. Opportunity, risks, chances, dangers, satisfaction, and purpose all lay before you. Every day will present you with new Goliaths which

you must face with the courage of your character. Otherwise, you can never be happy.

"But first, we must look to the day that will soon be dawning. Tomorrow, the traders and the buyers will fill the valley and crowd our tents and there will be much bargaining and many sales. Here we sit, in the midst of history and on the cusp of the brand-new morning. But first we must rest."

Stavros stood and lumbered toward the comfort of his wagon. I stayed there under the oak where we had spoken of courage and the future and I thought of ancient battles and adventures still to come until sleep overcame me.

The Next Name of Happiness

The Story of the Moonlight Ship

Crowds filled the marketplace *for the forty days we stayed in Elah. I learned the skills of trading and barter by following Stavros from tent to tent and from one transaction to the next. He mingled with the buyers and the sellers and engaged with each of them, making or refusing bargains.*

Each decision carried with it an element of risk and doubt even for the experienced merchant. Was his offer too low? Was the seller's demand too high? Would there be a market for the goods he considered? Would the next exchange be more to his advantage? Would the future bring a buyer for his merchandise? Each decision was a gamble against uncertainty. Every choice was infused with the risk of failure, and too many failures would risk the future of his enterprise. His business and his wealth, the labor of his hundred workers, his reputation as a man of skill and wisdom, all of these depended on his judgment and his knowledge, but more than that they depended on his courage. Day after day, as I followed him under the blazing sun, watching him make one split-second decision after another, I remembered the lesson he taught me on our first night in the valley. Courage brings happiness because it allows us to participate in our day-to-day affairs with confidence. When the evenings came and the bookkeepers made their tallies of the day's business, Stavros's smiles of achievement proved to me again and again that Courage is one of the Names of Happiness.

Finally, the time arrived for Stavros and his caravan to strike camp and head home. After many days of travel we were back at his headquarters in Phrygia and the workers began unloading his wagons and organizing the inventory of new goods for sale in the marketplace. He walked with me to the outskirts of the city. "I have never been to the Island of the Fisher King but its legends are well known in many of the villages and markets I have visited. The island is called Avalon and it is said that to reach it you must sail with the captain of the Moonlight Ship. He and he alone may land there. He and he alone can navigate the pathways that are drawn in the stars. You must travel east from here to the ancient port of Smyrna on the coast of Asia Minor and seek the Moonlight Ship. Tell the captain of your quest to learn the Names of Happiness and ask him to provide you with safe passage."

I embraced Stavros as a father and poured out words of thanks. He pressed a leather purse into my hands with a smile. "You will need some coins for food along the way. Travel safely, young friend. Act wisely and with courage." He turned and walked back to his market and I set out with the rising sun to guide my steps on the next leg of my voyage.

I walked for many days, sleeping in the open air and taking meals in the villages through which I passed. Finally, I smelled the salt air of the sea and knew the port was near. When I reached Smyrna I was amazed by the number of ships moored and anchored at the docks. I wandered aimlessly at first and then asked a sailor if he knew the Moonlight Ship. "Indeed I do," he answered and pointed toward the wind. "Her berth is straight ahead. I expect that you will know her when you see her."

And know her I did. True to her name, her hull was painted fore and aft with the color of a cloudless sky at night filled with the light of a full moon. Her sailors and crew were climbing the gangplank with sacks of provisions and the officers and mates stood on the top-deck looking out at the sea and then to their charts. It seemed as if I had reached her just in time to book passage. I jostled past the sailors to the deck and asked to see the captain.

He was younger than I expected, not many years older than me. His beard and hair were black and his face was smooth and unlined. "You would go to Avalon, you say?" He looked me up and down and reached into the pocket of his jacket. "I have a letter here from my friend, the Dragon Prince. He says that he has sent a traveler who seeks to meet the Fisher King. Would that be you?"

I was astonished that the prince had paved my way. "Yes. I have traveled far and wide, seeking to learn the Names of Happiness. May I . . ."

"Matthew!" he shouted. When a sailor ran to answer his call, the captain introduced us. "Matthew is my first mate. He will take you to your cabin. The voyage will be long and the waters can get rough." He gave me a wink and a smile. "But that should not

bother a traveler who has reached the Land Beside the Sky."

Matthew shook my hand and led me down some stairs. "Here is your cabin," he said when we reached an open door. "Come up onto deck in one hour's time and you may watch us start our voyage."

I took Matthew's advice and went topside to watch the ship leave port. The anchor was raised and we were untethered from our mooring. When we were free of our berth, the captain gave the order to set the topsails. A dozen sailors climbed the ship's three masts high above the deck. Each vertical mast had a horizontal timber attached as a giant cross a hundred feet aloft. The cross-masts held enormous bundles of canvas, gathered and tied with skeins of rope. The sailors walked away from the upright mast, balancing on ropes connected to the square rigging. I was horrified at the precariousness of their position, one false step and they would fall to certain death. But each of them pranced along the rope with ease and purpose. They were separate parts of a common effort, each one knew his place, and each one trusted his fellows to know theirs. When they were spread out across the width of the cross-masts the captain shouted his order: "Let fall the sails!" Every one of the sailors towering above me released one of the ropes which held the canvas to the mast, and then, like flowers blooming from their stems, the sails sprang from the bundles and fell free, hanging from the cross-masts until, with the merest hesitation, they filled themselves with the empty air around us as they caught the wind. In a moment we were off, cutting through the water like a swan.

I watched the sailors scamper down the masts and had not noticed that Matthew stood beside me. "The crew is never happier than when the sails are set and the ship launches itself into the wind. Look at their smiles." He was right. Each of the men who had descended the masts wore a broad grin and, once on deck, they warmly embraced one another. These men who had just risked their lives showed no signs of ever having been afraid. I had learned from Stavros that courage was one of the Names of Happiness, but I suspected that what I was watching here today carried a different meaning. I asked Matthew to explain.

"Do you see that sailor standing near the captain?" He pointed to a tall, young man, broad at the shoulder, lean and muscular. He had bright eyes and an easy grace as he went about his duties

winding rope lines. I recognized him as one of the men who had released the topsails to the wind. "His name is Samuel. He is the son of a prince of Africa. His family is wealthy beyond imagining and he been given every advantage of manhood and prosperity. He sails with the Moonlight Ship to experience the world. In time he will be a qualified mate, then a captain in his own right. One day he may command a navy. He has intelligence and nerve and he has mastered every job that a sailor may perform.

"But imagine if we had sent him aloft to the cross-mast all by himself. What then would have been the fate of our voyage? How would he have felt about his task? What would have been his mood, his frame of mind? And how successful would he have been at launching this great ship on its voyage to the future?

"A single man or woman, even the greatest sailor on Earth, would have failed dismally. And beyond the certainty of failure, that sailor would feel alone in the throes of danger, exposed to the contingencies of an uncertain world, vulnerable to every wobble of the mast, a solitary creature, dashing to and fro in a desperate attempt to succeed at an impossible task. And when the moment of

failure arrived, as certainly it would, the Moonlight Ship would be stranded at the dock, its sails uneven and insignificant, flapping in worthless futility."

I looked above at the sails filled with wind and felt the easy forward motion of the ship. Matthew was right. One man or woman alone could never have fulfilled the captain's command to let the sails fall. Even if some of the canvas was released and found the wind, the ship would have lurched and floundered. Miserable and beaten by the sea.

"I have read the captain's letter from the Dragon Prince," Matthew's words interrupted my musing. "And I know that you have made yourself a Voyager to find the Names of Happiness. Here is one that you must surely know: Friendship. This ship plies the waters of the world just as a single human life plies the currents of futurity. We are all mariners, sailing through the seas of time and space. None of us can set our sails alone or navigate the days of our existence without a friendly crew around us. A great philosopher has written that no person would choose to live without friends even if he or she possessed every other good thing that the world has to offer. Look at Samuel as the proof of that maxim. He has royalty and wealth and health and all advantages, but if he were friendless he

would fail—as a sailor and a person.

"The Moonlight Ship has no engine, friend Voyager. We have no oarsmen or steam. The motive force of this ship comes from the power of the atmosphere we live in. Your life and mine are like that. We travel from one day to the next, energized by the motor of the world. But friendless and alone, our paths would be confused and sad. It is with friendship that we set the sails of our own happiness, finding a fair wind and cutting through the expansive depths of life with spirit and bold hearts.

"Today you have learned that Friendship is a Name of Happiness."

"Matthew!" It was the captain's voice calling him to his duties. He smiled and dashed away with a bounce in his step. I knew that he and the captain and the crew, friends all, would land me safely on the shores of Avalon.

I opened the door to the Hikma Collection to find Clio sitting back in her chair with *The Seven Names of Happiness* open on the table. From where I stood I could hear her sobbing. I knew she must have read the name of friendship. Without taking a step closer, I spoke to her.

"That book is called *The Seven Names of Happiness*, young lady, not *The Key to Misery*." She turned at the sound of my voice and dabbed her teardrops with a tissue. She sniffled a little more as I walked over to her table. "What can there possibly be in those pages to make you feel so sad?" But, of course, I had always known the answer to that question.

"Mr. Atros, don't you see? The Story of the Moonlight Ship, it taught the Voyager that friends and friendships are important to happiness. The other Names of Happiness inspired me and gave me hope. I can be responsible. I can learn how to make wise choices; I can have courage and be grateful. But this—"

Then the sobbing started again.

"This one . . ." Sniffles.

"This one is . . ." Dabbing at the tears.

"This one is more than I can do. I am so very . . ." Her sobbing swallowed up the final word.

"Alone?" I offered.

She hid her face behind her hands and nodded

rapidly. "I am *so* very alone. I don't have any friends here. My parents are far away and there's no one for me to talk to. I came to Saga Street today to find a book to make me happy but instead of helping me be happy, this one explains why I have to be sad. I don't have any friends."

"Well thanks a lot," I laughed. "And here I thought you liked me." I sat in the chair beside her.

"I do like you. But I don't really *know* you and soon I'll have finished this book and the library will be closed."

"That's right, at six o'clock," I smiled.

Her eyes sprung open to twice their size and the words poured out her misery. "And then I'll go home to my empty apartment and then what?" She looked me directly eye-to-eye and said, "I'm lonely. Lonely and alone."

"More alone than the Voyager?" My question startled her. "You think that you're lonely because you have no one to talk to, because your familiar friends and your family are far away." I reached out and touched *The Seven Names of Happiness.* "But the Voyager journeyed all over the world and there is not a single sentence in that book that mentions a close friend or a family member. Have you gotten the impression that he was ever lonely?"

Her silence answered my question. "If you want

to understand the difference between being alone and being lonely answer this one question for me: What person was the most completely alone in all of human history?"

Clio had stopped sobbing. I could tell that she was thinking hard.

"I know that you don't mean the Voyager. That would be too easy. Sick people in hospitals have nurses and doctors to take care of them. Even prisoners in jail see the guards and other prisoners once in a while. Shipwrecked sailors or explorers who get lost in jungles? I don't think so. There are animals all around them." She thought harder and then her eyes lit up. She was sure she had the right answer.

"Adam!" she cried out. "Before Eve was created he was the only person in the world. No one else has ever been so alone and even the Bible says he was lonely." She smiled with the certainty that she was right. She wasn't.

"Not a bad guess," I said. "But Adam had God and all of creation to keep him company. The person I'm talking about was in many ways more commonplace than Adam, but in one very special way he was the most unusual man who ever lived.

"This man had studied to be a soldier and then trained to fly airplanes. He became a young test pilot at the beginning of the American space program and he applied to be part of that great adventure. His first application to be an astronaut was rejected, but he applied again and was accepted. On July 18, 1966 he orbited the Earth, walked in space, and returned safely three days later. His name is Michael Collins, and two years after his first space flight, on July 20, 1968, he became the most solitary person in all of human history.

"Here's how.

"Michael became the pilot of a space voyage called Apollo 11. It was humanity's first adventure to the surface of the Moon, the first time a human being would ever set foot on a celestial body other than the planet Earth.

"The voyage from the Earth to the Moon took three days and with Michael at the controls, the spacecraft named Columbia began orbiting the Moon in preparation for the final leg of the journey. On July 20 at about 6:00 p.m. Earth time, Michael's two fellow astronauts, Neil Armstrong and Buzz Aldrin, entered the lunar landing craft which would fly them to their destination on the surface, a spot called the Sea of Tranquility. A few hours later Neil Armstrong left the lunar module and became the first man to walk on the Moon. Moments later, Buzz Aldrin became the second."

Clio was confused. "What about Michael Collins?" she asked. "When did he walk on the Moon?"

"Michael Collins never walked on the Moon," I answered. "While Armstrong and Aldrin explored the lunar surface, Michael's job was to keep Columbia safely in orbit until they returned. For over twenty-one hours, Michael flew around and around the Moon all by himself. Armstrong and Aldrin were far below him. Every other human being was on Planet Earth, a quarter-million miles away. For half of his time in orbit, he was on the far side of the Moon which meant that he couldn't even radio anyone on Earth.

"We know how he felt during those dark moments because he kept a journal of his experiences. 'Far from feeling lonely or abandoned,' he wrote from the dark side of the Moon, 'I feel very much a part of what is taking place on the lunar surface. I am alone now, truly alone, and absolutely isolated from any known life. I am it. If a count were taken, the score would be three billion plus two over on the other side of the moon, and one plus God knows what on this side.'

"Michael Collins was alone for a very long time. He was more alone than any human being had ever been before. More alone than the Voyager. More alone by far, dear Clio, than you are. But he was never lonely. Not for a single minute.

"You see, loneliness is not the experience of being alone. It is a kind of pain that comes from our recognition that there is something missing from our life. Some part of human connection is absent. We look around ourselves and see that we are separated from our friends. Or maybe we feel as if we don't *have* any friends. Or maybe our friends are not committed to us in the ways we would like. These feelings of discomfort, vulnerability, isolation, and disconnectedness can have a thousand causes. They can result from many experiences of loss and insecurity. Each one makes us unhappy. But we don't have a thousand words for them, or even a hundred, so we tend to lump them all together and we call them loneliness.

"Feeling unloved is different than being physically alone, but people confuse them all the time.

"Feeling rejected by people whom we care about.

"Feeling different than the people around us.

"Feeling deprived of experiences of value.

"Being far away from the people who are most important to us.

"All of these feelings can become parts of the sorrow that we call loneliness. And believe me; none of them has anything in the world to do with being alone."

"You believe yourself to be lonely in the middle

of a bustling college campus, surrounded by hundreds of interesting people similar to you in age and circumstance, and attended to by hundreds of professors whose job it is to help you live a life of fulfillment and achievement.

"You feel the separation from your family, your old friends, your home and familiar places. That is a natural reaction for a person who has moved far away from familiar surroundings into a place that is new. Newness can feel strange, and strangeness can feel dangerous, and before too long you misidentify that strangeness as loneliness; and having given it that name you believe that your pain is on account of being alone."

I spread out my arms and smiled as broadly as I could. "Even when there are people all around you."

Clio was sitting back in her chair now staring straight at me as if she could listen with her eyes as well as her ears.

"That feeling that you call loneliness is actually a gift, a strange gift to be sure, but a gift nonetheless. It hides within a basic human need, pretending to be a problem while it actually serves an important purpose.

"Like hunger, the gift that tells you when you need to eat, or thirst, which tells you when you need to drink, loneliness tells you that you are starving yourself of connection and it urges you to engage openly with the world around you.

"We all need, and want, and deserve, connections with other human beings, with friends and family to be sure, but even with strangers and passers-by with whom we can share something as brief as a quick smile, or as simple as the humming of a happy tune.

"You were partly right about Adam a moment ago, Clio. He was not meant to live alone, that's not the reason his essence was introduced into this wonderful and complicated universe. I am old enough and have seen and learned enough to know that the same thing is true about everyone, even you. Especially you. You experience a feeling of distance from home, a lack of warm connections, a loss of friends and family. It makes you feel alone. It makes you feel isolated."

Clio was sniffling again. She wiped her nose and choked back a sob.

"But that's what I am. That's it exactly. I am isolated. I have become . . ."

"Nonsense," I interrupted. "Nonsense. You are not *isolated.* What you are is *insulated.* And you have done that to yourself."

It was time for some hard truths, and she needed to hear them. "You have wrapped yourself up in a cocoon. You have allowed your despair to cut you off from the fresh air of involvement with the world and instead you breathe toxic fumes of disappointment. No wonder you feel unwell, unhappy, and lonely. You are inhaling poison, the poisonous atmosphere of gloom.

"Remember that Michael Collins was sealed up in a steel capsule designed to protect him from the cosmic emptiness of outer space. He could have allowed himself to feel insulated—or isolated—from the wonders of the universe, but he didn't. Instead, he projected his soulfulness right through that steel shell and made himself part of the adventure playing out on the surface of the Moon.

"Later, when Aldrin and Armstrong were returning to Columbia, Michael took a photograph of their ship flying through space. The Moon itself was right beneath them and the Earth was floating in the distance. When that film was developed—yes, it was a long time ago and they still took pictures with film—someone realized that that single photograph contained, either actually or by memory, every living thing—people, animals, fish, birds, all the way down to insects, slugs, and bacteria—that lived or had ever lived on Earth, from the beginning of time right up to that very moment.

"Except for one. The only living being, alive or dead, present or past, that was not represented in that amazing photograph was Michael Collins himself, because he was behind the camera. He was the one taking the picture.

"Why didn't that make him feel isolated, sad, and lonely? Simply because while everyone else was in that frame, he was the only human being who was able to capture the experience of that moment. He and he alone could create that universe of meaning within the reach of his own unique vision.

"When he snapped the shutter that day, he was sealed off from every human being, but his act of creation connected him with everyone and everything that had ever lived. In that instant, in fact all throughout his solitary adventure, he was fully engaged with the universe. He made himself a star player in the drama of humanity."

"Do you think I can do that?" Clio's eyes were wide open and now they were free of tears.

"You are already doing it, my dear. You came to Saga Street today, you made a new friend," I put my hand over my heart when I said the word 'friend.' "And you are reading your Perfect Book at last."

"Perfect? At last? Come on, Mr. Atros. What's really going on here?"

I stood up from my chair. There were many things

I wanted to say to her, but I could see that she wasn't listening to me any longer. She had already turned the page to the next chapter of the book.

The Next Name of Happiness

The Story of the Storm at Sea

In the middle of our fourth night at *sea I was awakened by a crashing boom so loud that I expected to find that the Earth itself had been torn asunder. The ship rocked and swayed from side-to-side and when I left my hammock I could barely stand. In the pitch blackness of my cabin, I groped for the hallway door and held on to the wall in the darkness until I reached the top deck.*

The sky was filled with bolts of lightning and the air with bursts of thunder. Waves washed across the deck as the ship tilted and swayed right then left then right again, the crew members were sliding in the salt water and lurching from mast to mast.

"Hold fast, my friends. The sea is not yet finished with us." It was the voice of the captain and

in the next flash of lightning I saw him at the helm. His hands were clenched on the wheel and he struggled to keep his feet beneath him. "Steady, lads. We will ride the swells till morning."

His voice was strong and sure. He held fast to the wheel and steered the ship across every crest and wave. I clung for dear life to the frame of the door through which I had just passed and watched the captain's face in every gleaming flash of lightning. I'm sure that if anyone looked upon my face they would have known that I was terrified. The next wave could swamp the ship and send us to a watery doom. But I saw no terror on the face of the captain. His eyes were steady and his lips were pursed as if he were, and in the rare silent moments between thunder claps I could hear that he was indeed, whistling.

He turned his head to watch his crewmen following his commands and he glimpsed me shrinking in the darkness. "Ahoy, traveler," he shouted. "Keep your wits about you and stand firm. There's trouble enough tonight without you falling overboard and bothering the fish."

He turned back to the bow and held the ship on course for hour after hour, until darkness gave way to the dawn and the rolling water yielded to serenity.

Matthew took the wheel and the captain strode around the deck clasping the hands of his sailors and patting them on their backs. "Good work, brave lads. We have, it seems, another day before us."

I marveled at his cheer and his tranquility. In truth, my own knees were still weak from the peril of the night. But the captain walked the deck relaxed and at peace. He smiled wisely and was calm.

When he came again to me, he saw my look of wonder. "I suppose that was your first gale in the darkness of the sea?"

I nodded. "And I hope never to see another. All night I was seized by panic, while you stayed cool. How? I have learned on my travels that courage is one of the Names of Happiness, but your bravery . . ."

"You think it was bravery?" The captain shook his head. "It was not mere courage that kept the Moonlight Ship afloat above the waves. The sea cares not for courage and will sink the hero and the coward side-by-side. Happiness in the storm has a different name than courage."

I began to ask a question, but he raised his hand to silence me. "All in good time. Later we will speak of your next Name of Happiness. Until then, think of this—if I am as brave as a man must be to go to sea, then what about you? Here you stand with me right now, as we float together over the dangers of the deep. How is it then that we faced the challenge of the storm so differently?"

The captain turned and strolled to his cabin, leaving me alone to wonder at his words.

The sailing was peaceful on the fifth day. After the evening meal the captain and I stood upon the deck looking out over the smooth blue waters. He pointed at a spot of green barely visible on the horizon.

"That spot is the Island of the Fisher King and we shall reach its shores on the day after tomorrow. You will go upon your quest and I upon my next journey. I have sailed this passage many times and weathered many storms, and I shall sail it again. Does that surprise you?"

While I thought about his question, he asked me another. "What does it mean to you that you are alive and well and able to stand here with me and have a conversation aboard this ship?"

I didn't know what to say and the captain saw my confusion. "Here is what it means, my friend. Thus far in your life you have survived every day, every moment, every risk, and every peril of existence. You did not freeze to death finding the land of the Dragon Prince; you were not slain by highwaymen on your caravan to Elah. You neither starved nor lost your way on your journey to the Moonlight Ship in Smyrna. You have faced other moments when danger confronted you or hardship showed its face; but here you are, having beaten every one."

I listened carefully to the captain's words and thought about the desperate moments that inspired my first voyage. "And more than that," he continued, "cast your imagination back through the ages—to every one of your ancestors, fathers and mothers, all of whom lived and flourished long enough to produce the next generation of children who then went on to produce the next and the next one after that. In ancient times, the risks to life were greater even than the ones we face today. The lives of all our forebears, just as my life and yours, indeed just like the life of every living soul, has been a journey over rough seas as well as calm ones. And yet," he waved his hand to encompass the entire ship upon which we stood, "we continue to set our sails for tomorrow, we embark upon the voyages of destiny. Why?"

I thought I had the answer. "Because we hope for the best?"

"Hope? Is that what you believe?" The captain chuckled. "What is hope but a wish that the future will unfold according to our desires? Would I dare to sail the seas of peril if I bound my future with such a fragile thread as hope? No. The Moonlight Ship and I bind our prospects and our happiness with stronger stuff than that. Optimism is your next Name of Happiness: that confident expectation that the world of good fortune which has carried us this far will not shipwreck us on the rocky throes of failure."

I must have seemed unconvinced. "But . . ." I started.

"But, indeed. Think beyond your own life and lineage. Look to the life of our species, the life of humanity, and every one of its meaningful endeavors. At every turn, the history of mankind has been the optimistic achievement of greater and greater accomplishment. Think about science: has the march toward knowledge crashed on beaches of ignorance? No. It advances by every generation until our understanding dwarfs the knowledge of the ancients.

"What about medicine? Do the healers of today know less than their teachers?

"Or exploration? Have the world and the stars shut themselves off from the searching pioneers?

"Philosophy? Poetry? Business? Education? Of course you know the answers. The life of our world, no more or less than the world of our lives, advances from greatness to higher greatness. This is not a matter of simple hope. It is the lesson of every yesteryear and the promise of tomorrow. It is Optimism that launches my ship upon the waves, and optimism that encourages me with cheer when the ocean boils with danger. I have weathered many storms and I expected, I believed, that I would weather last night's too."

Now I had to speak. The captain was certainly forgetting a simple fact of life. "But Captain, many ships do not reach their destination. The journals of the news are filled with accounts of vessels dying in the sea. What did optimism do to preserve those sailors?"

"You are right, of course; but your question proves my point. When a ship goes down it is a newsworthy event because it is unusual and only because of that. Only the rare voyage ends in misfortune. You worry about the world of evil and occasional hardship and wonder if we are foolish to

practice optimism.

"We would certainly be foolish to expose ourselves to certain danger or to look for witless prospects of good fortune. I am optimistic at the wheel of my ship, but I nonetheless steer clear of the rocks and whirlpools. Optimists do not ignore peril or vicissitudes of fate, but we look at our current situations in the best possible, most realistic, light, and we expect a future of happiness. Optimism allows us to feel positive in our relationships with others and gives us the responsibility to practice courage and gratitude. Every waking morning is an occasion for thanksgiving. Every night that you lay your head on the pillow, your restful sleep is a cause for happiness.

"You have a choice to see the world in a positive or negative light. You may choose to avoid optimism and expect the world to fall apart tomorrow, and you can fear the drawing of every breath. But would that make you happier? After all, tomorrow is known to no one. Scientists and scholars have proven that our memories do not even tell us the whole truth about what has happened in the past. If we cannot know the past with certainty, how much more foolish is it to believe that we can know the

future? To be wise, we embark on the voyages of life expecting to reach the destinations of our dreams. We can, if we wish, doubt our arrival and sail in fear and torment, much as you were in the storm last night. But I do not believe that such a course would make you happy."

The Moon was full that night and it was high in the sky. The sailors of the night watch had taken their stations. I was tired after my sleepless night and I yawned.

"We will go to our cabins soon, but first let me tell you about a time that a baby was born in the land of America. She was a beautiful child given to loving parents. But just as some ships sink at sea, the joy of the parents sank when their child suffered an illness that stole her hearing and her sight. She spent many years locked in darkness and silence, in absolute isolation. Only after meeting a dedicated teacher did she gain the power to communicate and understand language.

"How much more reason has anyone ever had to be a pessimist? She could have lived out a life without hope or expectation of happiness. Instead, she took responsibility for her future, engaged in the world around her, became the friend of writers and

of scientists, and at the age of twenty-three, when she was a student in college, she wrote a short book in which she recorded the evil that had befallen her and proclaimed that she could still have a positive expectation that good things lay ahead—in spite of everything she suffered. Her name was Helen Keller.

"Helen Keller knew that the chronicles of human history as surely as the story of her own life must teach us to be optimists."

The captain and I headed for the decks below. "That is why, when I set my sails to my next voyage, I will choose to be optimistic. I have my knowledge of the sea and my faith in the future and I will expect once again to reach my destination."

When we came to my cabin, the captain patted my shoulder. "Thirty more hours of sailing will take us to Avalon, and your next lesson of happiness."

She was sitting straight up in her chair with her arms crossed, deep in thought, when I opened the door.

When she finally noticed me standing there the question burst out of her. "The book says that the Voyager traveled through space and time. How is that possible? I mean, it isn't—is it? For someone to travel through space and time would take . . ."

She grew silent, not wanting to say the word.

"Magic?" I finished her thought and smiled. "You know, there are many different ideas about magic. Some people believe that there are sorcerers who can turn lead into gold. Others believe that they can turn night into day. I don't think any of that is true. But I do believe that there is a real kind of magic. A magic that involves transformation, a change that comes upon us that is so extraordinary and unexpected that we cannot explain it other than by wondering about the strangeness of the world.

"There is proof of that right here in this room." The book that had taken up so much of my life still lay open on the table and I touched it gently. "This morning you came to Saga Street lonely and unhappy. You despaired of happiness and wished, without believing, that you would find a book to change your life. And then you found *The Seven Names* and you began unfolding into a confident young woman who knows the Names of

Happiness and can learn how to call them forth into her life. What is that if not a transformation? What is that if not magic?

"It's been a pleasure finally to meet you, Clio," I said as I stood beside her table. "But I have come here to say good night. I'll be leaving Saga Street soon. I have to start a long voyage and there a few errands for me to attend to before I go." I gently patted her shoulder and turned for the door.

"Wait!" she called out. "What do you mean 'finally' meet me? What is the meaning of all of this?"

I looked down at the book on the table. "You still have more to read and not much time left," I said. "It's almost six o'clock. I had better not disturb you any longer."

"Okay, so you won't tell me what 'I'm glad to finally meet you' means. How about answering this question: I've been in this town a whole semester and I go downtown a lot. There is no café called Sophie's. Why not?"

I sat down again, across the table from her. "No there isn't. After Sophie opened the library she came here every evening for about six months. At first she was working on the Hikma Collection, selecting the books that would go in this room. After that, she used to sit downstairs and read and look around at what Doctor Hikma's vision had created. Then one day she didn't visit Saga Street anymore. The sign in her café's window which had always said 'Open your eyes with the best coffee in town' was replaced by another that said 'For Sale. Reasonable Terms.' A couple of young attorneys bought the place and turned it into their office. After that, Sophie disappeared, leaving her friends to wonder where she had gone. Some remembered that she had always wanted to study painting in Europe. Others thought she must have taken the around-the-world cruise she used to talk about. Nobody knew for sure, but some folks were saying that it was pretty strange that so many people were disappearing all of a sudden. It was downright eerie.

"When the lawyers who bought the café started clearing out Sophie's storage room they came across an old oil painting of Doctor Hikma as a young man. No telling where Sophie had gotten her hands on it. They donated it to the library and it's been hanging downstairs behind the circulation desk ever since. Maybe you noticed it when you walked in."

Clio shook her head.

"No? Well, no matter. Take a look at it when you leave. Pretty handsome fellow if you ask me."

Clio sat up a little straighter in her chair. "What did the letter say?"

"Letter?"

"You said that Doctor Hickma's 'Read This' envelope contained a deed, a key, and a letter. What did the letter say?"

"Ah. Well now, Clio, many people have asked that very question. The truth is that Sophie never told anyone about it. As for Doctor Hikma, I suppose that if he wanted the letter to be a matter of public knowledge he wouldn't have sealed it up tight inside that envelope."

I stood up and glanced again at *The Seven Names on Happiness*. "I envy you the experience of reading this for the first time. But now I really do have to go."

"I'll be coming back to the library a lot from now on," said Clio. "I guess I'll see you again when you get back from your trip."

I just smiled, opened the door, and walked slowly down the stairs. Clio had one more chapter to read in her Perfect Book.

The Next Name of Happiness

The Story of the Fisher King

***The captain of the Moonlight Ship** spread out a parchment map of the Island of Avalon. It showed a winding river and broad plains. In the center of the island was a castle. The ink on the map had faded with the ages but I could still read the words that the map-maker had written. "Here resides the Fisher King."*

The captain placed his finger near those words. "Your quest for the next Name of Happiness must take you here, friend traveler, to the castle of the Fisher King." He folded the map carefully and handed it to me. "Carry this with care. It is the only map of Avalon. I trust you to use it well and wisely."

The next morning the captain brought his ship safely to land. His sailors jumped onto the dock and tied thick ropes from the bow and stern to mooring cleats and made the ship rest still. I disembarked with the parchment map and walked off to the west.

When I reached the winding river I saw a humble boatman straining with deep breaths to beach his tiny boat. His hair and beard were gray, his tunic old and tattered. At the edge of the water he stepped off onto the sand and dragged his boat ashore.

"Ahoy, friend visitor," said the boatman. "What brings you here to Avalon?" He staggered towards me and looked me up and down. "Your clothes are not from here and you carry a traveler's pack. Have you come to meet the king?" The old man leaned forward and spoke to me in a whisper. "Are you questing for his treasure?"

"I am a Voyager from far away," I answered. "The captain of the Moonlight Ship brought me to the shores of this island and told me to follow this map to the king and to his castle."

"Ah, the map," smiled the boatman. "You have the map. Well then, we will travel to the place

you seek but you must pull the oars and pay the price of your adventure."

"But I have no money," I said, and I thought my quest would end there in defeat.

"The price of your quest cannot be paid with money," said the boatman. "You must pay it with a question." My face betrayed my confusion and the boatman spoke again. "We need not settle the matter now." He pointed to the west where I could see the tallest spires of the castle, sparkling through the mist.

He stepped back into his boat and I pushed it free of the shore and jumped in. I pulled at the oars with all my might and soon we were gliding through blue water. The castle grew clearer with every moment. My mind was filled with questions. What was the price that the boatman would have me pay? And how could I pay it with a question? I pulled the oars and wondered.

"You must be thirsty from your rowing," said the boatman, and he took from his tunic's pocket a simple glass bowl. He dipped it in the water and I took the bowl and drank it.

"Good, good," whispered the boatman. "The water has refreshed you," and he dipped and drank himself. "We must walk the rest of the way to the

castle. Bring the boat ashore and we will continue on your quest." I rowed the boat to the riverbank and jumped onto dry land. I pulled the boat aground, helped the boatman step ashore, and together we looked off to the west toward the castle gates.

The boatman had taken a walking stick from the boat and he leaned on it for support. I slowed my gait so that the two of us walked side by side.

"We have a ways to go," said the boatman. "An hour, maybe more. That gives me time to tell you about this place and how it came to be."

"My name is Bron, and when I was myself as young and strong as you, I made my living fishing in these waters. I slept on my boat or in the caves throughout the hillsides. My parents had long ago been gathered, and I had neither brothers nor sisters. My friends were other fishers and the merchants to whom I sold my catch. Otherwise, I was alone until the day that I met Artemis, the daughter of Erasmus the cod fisher. The first time I saw her she was sitting on that rock right there, the same one I now point to. The sun was hot and high. She had returned from a fishing trip with her father's crew and was resting in the warmth of noon. Erasmus approached her and they spoke in laughs and whispers. He called me over

to them and I went. Artemis stood and stretched, and dazzled in the sun.

"We married at the sixth full moon thereafter according to the rituals of the island. Erasmus and his wife Ruth were witness to our happiness. Artemis's sisters and brothers were there too, including her brother Joseph, a tin merchant from the far-off land of Judah. His home was at a crossroads of the trade routes, a town which some called Ramah, and others called Zophim. But most people knew it as Arimathea, which means the city of disciples.

"Since that day Artemis and I have enjoyed many years of happiness. We fished and built our home together, and we grew old side by side. One day her brother Joseph traveled here again from Judah. His visit was a blessing after so many years apart. He brought us gifts of tinware from his warehouse, and also gold and silver. Incense, spices, jewels, and rugs filled his wagon and when all had been unloaded Artemis and I marveled at the treasures.

"We carried the gifts into every room of our home until Joseph held only a simple canvas bundle, wound up and tied with twine."

He held his hands apart to measure the span of one man's hand. "Joseph's bundle was no bigger than this. But when I asked to know its contents, he said that within the canvas was a prize more precious than all the goods and jewels and tin he had brought us from afar. 'Let us sit and eat,' he said, 'and speak no more about it.'

"Artemis and I prepared a feast of tuna, breads, and cheeses from the village. As we made the meal ready, Joseph described his journey from Judah and the dangers he had faced along the way. We praised him for his courage and his skill. He quieted us with a wave of his hand.

"'Without expedition there is no fulfillment,' he said. 'Without voyages of discovery, there can be no happiness.'"

Then Bron turned to me with a look both stern and kind. "Have you learned that lesson, friend stranger? Have you truly been a Voyager?"

I straightened, no longer tired, and answered in a clear voice. "I left my home fires long ago to seek the secrets of the world and the stars. In every land I have visited, I have studied the ways of men and women who know the Names of Happiness and sorrow. I have written all the things I learned on parchment and on vellum and I carry them all with me in my bag. The Dragon Prince sent me here to Avalon to learn the secrets of the Fisher King. Will you help me find that knowledge?"

The words rushed from my lips, fast and hopeful. My aged guide just smiled and returned to his story.

"After we had eaten our fill, Joseph told us about a man from his homeland who had been murdered for teaching lessons filled with wisdom and love. Joseph had admired the great teacher and wanted to give him a proper burial. He claimed his body and wrapped him in a linen shroud. He laid him to rest in a tomb cut in a cave. He hired workers to seal up the cave with a great rock to protect it from robbers.

"'The next week I traveled to an upper room,' said Joseph, 'a place where the teacher's followers were gathered, so that I might share their grief and offer whatever help my wealth could give.'

"'We need nothing,' said their leader. 'We do not grieve our teacher for he is no longer dead. He has returned and lives among us. He visits us and preaches throughout the land, even now spreading his message of love and understanding.'

"Joseph could scarcely believe their words. He had held the lifeless form and felt the coldness of death's chill. But so adamant where they, and not prone to deception, that he had no choice but to accept their words as true. He shouted with joy and sat down at their table exhausted with emotion. Joseph paused his story there and placed his small canvas bundle on our own table. 'Before me on the table there was this.'

"With those words he loosed the twine and unwrapped the package. It held a plain glass bowl just large enough to drink from. 'When the teacher visited his followers he drank from this very bowl,' said Joseph. 'The leader of the disciples saw me admire it and he offered it to me as a gift for my kindness. I have carried it with me ever since.'

"He slid it across the table to his sister and to me. 'It is a thing of wonder and great power. For the worthy seeker after wisdom, a sip from this bowl bestows long life, a mastery of space and time, and the greatest gift of happiness. I entrust it now to you to keep it safe and sound and secret. Share it only with those who are worthy and deserve to receive its gifts.'

"Joseph stayed with us for seven more days and nights, and then packed his wagon and headed home to Judah. He dwells there still, protected and enlivened by the blessings given to him by the bowl. He lives on to an ancient age and does good deeds for everyone he meets.

"As for Artemis and I, we have protected the bowl and guarded its secrets for many, many years."

By now we had reached the castle doors. They opened into a great hall with a table filled with meats and fruits and breads from every land. A woman with long gray hair and a robe that glistened green and purple rose from a couch to greet me. She took my hand in both of hers and must have noticed my bewilderment.

"Greetings to you, dear Voyager," she said with a voice of harp strings and gentle winds. "We have been waiting for you for a very long time."

I turned upon the man whom I had known simply as a boatman. "Then you are . . ."

"Yes," he smiled. "I am the Fisher King. Welcome to our castle and to Avalon."

We spent a long evening beside the fire of the castle's massive hearth. The king and queen, Bron and Artemis, told me of the many searchers for the glass bowl: some worthy, others not. For many years they had followed Joseph's admonition and kept it safe and sound.

"The hour grows late, dear traveler. The time has come for you to pay the price of your quest." I remembered that the Fisher King, when I saw him as a simple boatman, told me that I must pay for my adventure with a question. But what should the question be? And if I asked the wrong one, what then? He sensed my apprehension.

"You have scoured the world for the Names of Happiness and your quest has brought you here. Have you noticed in your travels that those two words—quest and question—have the same root? They both speak of discovery, of enlarging one's soul by exposing it to the universe of knowledge all around us. Have you done that, my friend? Have you opened up your soul to the world around you? Have you made yourself a student of discovery?"

The king's words brought a tear to my eye as I recalled my travels, from my home to the realm of the Dragon Prince to the city of King Midas and the rest. "I have tried, dear King. I have quested for the lessons of the Earth and the stars and I have learned many things. But now I wonder. How can I best teach those things to others and share with them the lessons which heal sorrow and despair?"

Queen Artemis smiled at the Fisher King and then at me.

"You have asked well, young Voyager. Your wise question has paid your fare to Avalon and it has paid for your draught from the cup of wisdom."

"Yes," I cried, unable to contain my excitement. "Let me behold the glass and drink from it."

The king drew from the pocket of his tunic the same small bowl that he had dipped into the water of the river.

"That? Is that—" I could scarcely understand.

"Your spirit of discovery has earned you the draught of wisdom. The captain of the Moonlight Ship is our son, and he knows our secret. The map he gave you is the sign by which we identify seekers on a worthy quest."

Artemis laid her hand on her husband's and spoke to me. "He brought you here and sent you with the map so that you might drink from Joseph's bowl. Some have called the bowl a Sacred Chalice or the Vessel of Wisdom. But we know it as the Grail and we have discovered that it will bring you gifts bounded only by your merit and by your willingness to help others."

"Everything you deserve, but only that and nothing more." Bron stood and I knew that our evening had reached its end. "Today you have learned that the Spirit of Discovery is the greatest Name of Happiness. Now you must decide how to use that knowledge." The queen rose from her seat and the two of them left me by the fire wondering about the future. If indeed my discoveries would give me long life and wisdom, how would I live that life so as to deserve those gifts? The riddle kept me awake throughout the night.

When Bron and Artemis re-entered the great hall with the rising sun I was still seated next to the dwindling embers of the fire. Artemis spoke to me with a gentle voice. "Have you settled on an answer, young friend? What will you discover next?"

I stood and gave them both an embrace of friendship and farewell. I took one last look at the great hall of the Fisher King and at the table that held the Grail.

I strode then with new confidence beyond the castle doors and made my way back to the berth of the Moonlight Ship. With a smile I returned to the captain the map drawn on a sheet of parchment which might someday guide another worthy traveler. We sailed to a port that lay beyond the Inland Sea where I disembarked with just my bag and the promise of tomorrow.

I wandered far and wide and then settled down at a place beside a stream and a meadow where I built a house of fieldstone and cedar. Friendships, and then families, and a village grew around me. The children thought me very old but to their parents I seemed as young as new ideas. In time my house became a place for learning and I taught what I had found throughout my travels: lessons of loving peace, making art, having health, and walking the path of bliss.

In time, I left that town and found another. I became a healer and a teacher, and passed along the stories of my voyages so that everyone could know the wondrous Names of Happiness.

Part Three

The Second 'Read This' Letter

Chapter Five

CLIO AND THE LIBRARIAN

Clio just sat there for a few moments, trying to process all she had read. She hadn't noticed that the daylight had grown dim outside the windows, but evening came early in January and now the Moon was full and the stars were bright against the sky. The reading lamp on the table cast a cone of light around the book that was spread in front of her, opened to its last page. She was so absorbed in her own thoughts that she didn't hear the door open behind her.

"Excuse ME, young lady! I don't know how you got into this room but this collection is private, just like the sign says. Not open to the public. It's a good thing I decided to check before we locked up for the night."

The librarian—she must be a librarian, thought Clio—flipped a switch and bathed the room in brightness.

She seemed very old to Clio, but young people often do misjudge age. Her gray hair was pulled into a ponytail and her bright plaid skirt and turtleneck sweater made her look like, well, rather like Clio might look someday.

She walked toward the table and then noticed the glass case with its open lid.

"Oh dear! However did you open that case? It should have been locked and . . ." Then she looked at the blue leather book in front of Clio.

"*The Seven Names!* That volume is never allowed out of its case. It is the jewel of the Hikma Collection. Very old. Very fragile. She closed it very carefully and lifted it from the table, holding it close to her chest.

"I think you had better tell me exactly what you are doing here and how you came to be reading this particular book."

Clio was worried by the librarian's harsh tone. Was she in trouble? How could she be when Mr. Atros brought her to this room, unlocked it with his key, and then opened the display case?

"I'm sorry if I've done anything wrong," she said. "I came this morning to find a book that might help me start the New Year without being as sad and lonely as I've been. Mr. Atros saw me and said that he could always pick the Perfect Book for everyone. He's the one who brought me up here and gave me this book to read, and he was right. It's wonderful. I've never read anything like it. But there is no title page, no author's name anywhere. Do you know who wrote it?"

The librarian examined Clio more carefully than before but she didn't answer her question. "So far as anyone knows this is the only copy of *The Seven Names* in existence. Scholars from across the globe have traveled here to study it. They have taken its message home with them to the four corners of the Earth. The lessons of this book have changed countless lives, even with the mystery of the missing chapter."

"Missing chapter?" It seemed to Clio as if the room was spinning.

"Yes, you must have noticed that in spite of its title the book describes only *six* Names of Happiness."

"Six names!" Clio hadn't noticed that. The chapters weren't numbered and she had been so enthralled by her reading and her conversations with Mr. Atros that she hadn't counted them.

The librarian continued. "Some people believe that the book is a riddle, a mathematical conundrum."

"What do *you* think?" asked Clio.

The librarian paused. "I believe that the Seventh Name of Happiness is different for every individual. The nature of the Seventh Name depends on why you needed to read the book in the first place and on the particular lessons you take away from it." Then she smiled for the first time since Clio met her. "But I believe that there is another mystery that we should try to solve first."

Clio looked at the librarian in confusion. "What do you mean?" she wondered.

"Simply this," answered the librarian. "Who in the world is Mr. Atros?"

Chapter Six

CLIO AND THE PORTRAIT

"Who is . . . Well he is . . ." Clio could barely speak. Who was Mr. Atros? Well he was the wisest man Clio had ever met. But more than that, mustn't he be an important librarian on Saga Street in order to have keys to the private room and the case that held *The Seven Names*? Now Clio was more curious than ever. What exactly had happened today?

"I think perhaps you'd better come down-stairs with me." The librarian walked to the door and waited with the book still in her hands. "It's six o'clock and I would like to close the library on time."

Clio stood and nervously followed her into the hallway. The librarian turned off the lights and locked the door with a big brass key, just like the one that Mr. Atros had used.

Clio followed her down the stairs to the circulation desk. Then she saw it.

"They came across an old oil painting of Doctor Hikma as a young man," he had told her. "It's been hanging downstairs behind the circulation desk. Pretty handsome fellow if you ask me."

And there he was. The picture was hanging right where he had said it would be. A huge oil painting. Six feet high at least. The portrait of a young man, older than Clio, but not by much. He stood with his left hand in the pocket of his corduroy pants. His tweed jacket looked brand new in those days, and his hair and beard were still black. His green eyes still twinkled and his glasses were pushed up atop his head. There was a wall of bookcases behind him and he was standing on an Arabian rug. She was sure that it was the same one she had just seen in the reading room upstairs.

The man's right hand held a book with a blue leather binding. It must have been *The Seven Names of Happiness*. She couldn't be totally sure, of course, but there was one thing about which she was positive.

"That man. In the painting. It's Mr. Atros. Surely you must know him. He works here in the library and there he is and . . ."

The librarian spoke with a friendly voice. "The man in that portrait is Isaac Hikma. Doctor Hikma was the benefactor of the Library on Saga Street and the man in whose book collection you found *The Seven Names*. The portrait was painted in the doctor's library and it has been hanging in that spot for a very long time; almost ever since the library was dedicated nearly a hundred years ago."

"You mean when the mayor and the governor were here and when Sophie cut the ribbon." Clio remembered Mr. Atros's story.

"Why yes." The librarian seemed to get lost in a memory. "That was a happy day for everyone."

Clio walked a few steps closer until she stood right in front of the painting. There was not a single doubt in her mind. She turned to face the librarian. "He told me his name was Isaac. Isaac Atros. This is the man who took me upstairs and gave me *The Seven Names*. 'I can always recommend the Perfect Book,' he said. But . . . A hundred years ago? He was here today. As alive as you and me. He changed my life. How . . ."

She ran to the librarian and grabbed the book from her. "He knew that books can change lives and that this one would change mine. He was here. He knew."

"It seems that someone played a joke on you." The librarian's voice was very soft now. "If you shortened that name to its first initial then Isaac Atros becomes I. Atros, which becomes iatros. *Iatros* is the Greek word for doctor. For a physician like . . ."

"Like him," Clio cried out as she pointed to the painting. "He was giving me clues all day. The library. The book. His name. Don't you see? That's Mr. Atros! I don't know how it's possible. But he knew that I needed his help. He knew I needed to read this book. He knew it would be . . ."

Before she could say "The Perfect Book," the rear cover of the book fell open just a crack and an envelope fluttered to the floor. Clio was positive that it hadn't been there when she was upstairs, reading it from cover to cover.

The librarian bent over and picked it up. She looked at it, looked at the portrait of Doctor Hikma, and then handed the envelope to Clio who gave the book back to her. "I had better put this back where it belongs," she said as she headed back up the stairs. "I guess I won't be closing the library at six o'clock tonight."

The bewildered girl looked at the envelope. There were three words written on its face.

Clio. Read This.

And so she did.

Chapter Seven

THE SECOND 'READ THIS' LETTER

My Dear Clio,

I hope that you will excuse my little subterfuge and the bad pun.

Isaac Atros. Iatros. Doctor Hikma. Those are a few of the names by which I have been known over a life both long and full. I have also been called the Teacher, the Wise One, the Philosopher, and yes, the Voyager. To many people I have been a traveler and a builder and a healer, but today I appeared to you as a librarian in this place of wisdom that once had been my home.

There are tens of thousands of books within these walls, and tomorrow there will be other books for you to read, and in the days and years to come still more. But I knew that The Seven Names of Happiness was the right one for you today. At this moment of your life, when you felt sadness and despair and loneliness, it was your Perfect Book.

How did I know that? And why did I expect to meet you here today? And why is its lesson so perfect for whoever reads it?

Those are all good questions and I know that you would like them answered. But first, the title. By now you know that The Seven Names of Happiness has only six chapters. The Seventh Name is different for every reader, but every seventh name hides among the six you've already read about, and becomes the last lesson of the voyager. I reserve it for those who deserve the transformational magic of its wisdom.

And now I give you your very own Seventh Name of Happiness. It is this:

Kindness.

What is kindness? It is a practice and a state of mind.

It is the art of giving goodness to others without any hope or expectation of a benefit in return.

It is the expression of a hopeful wish that other people may live free from suffering. It is the habit of helping them find peace. It is a blessing of compassion and fulfillment.

To be kind is to live in sympathy with your community; to experience the pleasures of the world around you; to extend a spirit of friendship, caring, understanding, appreciation, and respect.

Every act and thought of kindness is an act and

thought of generosity that reaches beyond the walls of our identity and takes advantage of the infinite opportunities to add brightness and inspiration to the universe. Being kind we project our individuality into the great adventures of life around us: the day-to-day journeys of quests and questions.

Whenever we pay attention to the humanity of another person and his or her most basic need, to be appreciated and noticed, that moment of intentional awareness is a moment of kindness. Our involvement in the enduring continuity of life connects us to eternity and it gives the world a weapon with which to ward off cruelty and heartlessness.

You see, dear friend, life imposes upon us the responsibility to live it. We are ordained to be part of the Grand Scheme of Completeness, the mundane and wonderful organism of the cosmos.

Clio raised her eyes from Mr. Atros's letter.

Courage.

Discovery.

Connection.

Responsibility.

Gratitude.

This was all starting to sound very familiar.

She kept reading.

That's right, Clio. Kindness is more than just The Seventh Name of Happiness. It is all of Happiness itself, the entirety of fulfillment.

I wish I could take the credit for the wisdom that kindness is a weapon against cruelty, but that belongs to a fifteen-year-old girl who wrote it in her diary one day in 1943.

That girl lived with her family in Amsterdam. She had a mother and a father and a sister who was three years older than her. Her father was a businessman and he had a secretary named Miep Gies.

Mrs. Gies seemed an unremarkable woman. She was thirty-four years old. She had grown up poor and often went hungry because her family could not afford to feed her. When she was eleven years old, her parents sent her to live with strangers so that she could have, at least, basic food and shelter. She studied hard, became an honor student in high school, and at the age of eighteen got her first real job. Later, she became the secretary to the manager of a pectin factory. The manager's name was Otto Frank.

At that moment of history, the Nazi terror of

hatred and cruelty was sweeping across Europe and Jewish people like Otto Frank's family were being hunted, targeted for certain death. If the Nazi police arrested them, they would be doomed.

So Otto and his wife, their two children, and some friends hid in the attic rooms above Otto's office. In order to survive there, they needed someone to bring them food, to keep their secret, to help them stay alive. Someone had to reach outside the container of their own isolation and pay attention to the humanity of the Frank family, to honor and respect their membership in the eternal fellowship of connection. For over two years, that someone was Mrs. Gies.

If the Nazis discovered what she was doing she would be in grave danger and that awareness must have been terrifying. But she had been hungry, she understood the pain of deprivation, and she knew the anguish of uncertainty. Putting her life on the line, she cast aside the comfortable falsehood that came so easily to many others that she was not part of world around her, and she replaced her fear of cruelty with the power of kindness and courage.

Eventually, Otto's family and friends were discovered and arrested. Mrs. Gies's victory over evil was temporary. Nonetheless, she had given the Frank family two more years of life together. Two years in which, while they were deprived of comfort and a normal existence, they could feel hope that there was still some good remaining in a world gone mad.

How do we know all this? We know it because one of Otto's daughters, that fifteen-year-old girl whom I mentioned earlier, recorded her feelings during those months of hiding. She wrote in a journal that her father had given her for her thirteenth birthday, and when she had filled that journal she wrote on whatever scraps of paper she could find. She wrote down her thoughts of bravery and optimism and her understanding of the ultimate decency of humanity.

And then, long before her story should have ended, she was swept away and murdered by a cruelty so profound and terrible that it has ever since been known by one awful and terrifying name: Holocaust.

That journal and those scraps of paper survived because Miep Gies discovered them in the attic and saved them in a desk drawer. Otto Frank survived the Holocaust and Miep Gies gave his daughter's writings to him. They were published as a book, a chronicle of the human spirit that inspires the world. Millions of people in every generation have read that short book and its anecdotes of wisdom and sincerity, written in the midst of fear and misery by a short-lived Voyager who nonetheless believed that people were really good at heart and that the world remained a beautiful place. That message may not yet have changed the entire world but it changes the life of anyone who reads it. For many people, it is their Perfect Book. We have of it here at Saga Street and if you haven't read it you really should. Its proper name is The Diary of a Young Girl, but most people call it The Diary of Anne Frank.

Miep Gies could have looked the other way and allowed inhumanity to prevail; many, many others did exactly that. When her heroism became well known she was pronounced Righteous Among the Nations, kings and commoners alike lavished her with praise and adoration. But what did she say about herself? "I am not a special person," she declared. "I did what any decent person would have done."

What had she done, exactly? She had involved herself in the story of the universe. She discovered an opportunity to change the world for the better and she gratefully accepted that opportunity. She acted with the courage of her moment. She recognized her responsibility to be part of the human condition, and the consequences of her actions have resonated around the globe.

In other words, she was kind. And her kindness has spread happiness throughout the world.

Ah, but what about optimism? Does that Name of Happiness fit into the definition of kindness?

Remember this, Clio. Kindness needs an object. It needs someone to receive it just as much as it needs someone to perform it. There is no such thing as kindness in a vacuum. It is always a gift that passes from the giver to the recipient. Kindness needs a beneficiary, someone it can help.

And the first and most important beneficiary of your kindness must always be yourself.

Never save all of your love, acceptance, understanding, and forgiveness for others. You deserve some of it yourself. In fact, you deserve a lot of it yourself. Be kind to yourself by casting aside pessimism, despair, self-condemnation, and worry. Live a life of joyful expectation.

Optimism energizes your power to be kind to others. With optimism, we audaciously discover every good thing that the universe offers us and we explore the goodness of creation. We expose ourselves to the opportunities of benevolence. The next hour, the next day, or month, or year might not give you everything you wish for. But they might. Either way, as long as you can breathe the fresh air of hope, you are free to wish anew. Optimism completes The Seventh Name of Happiness.

But you may still be wondering how a man from so very long ago and so very far away would come to Saga Street today to lead you up a flight of stairs simply to show you your Perfect Book. Allow me to tell you one more story before the library closes on your New Year's Day.

The Story of the Plague

The Origin of The Voyager

There was a time when plague swept throughout the world *until it reached the land where a young man lived alone.*

He had seen the plague approaching, and so he laid in a store of supplies and food to sustain him while he sheltered in his house of bricks and mortar, hiding from the sickness that raced around the countryside leaving death and fear and sadness in its wake.

The plague moved slowly, lingering in the young man's village for many months. The young man's fellow villagers remained cloistered, locked against the pestilence, weeping in their isolation, and fearing for their loved ones. Whenever he dared to open his shutters he could hear the moaning of the sick and the anguished sobs of the lonely.

The plague brought more than fever to the land; it brought terror and despair, separation, hunger, poverty, and woe. Workers and artisans abandoned their studios. Farmers left their fields. The marketplace, once busy and crowded with buyers and with sellers, became deserted. Wagons stopped bringing goods to market as the drivers fell ill. Even horses and oxen took the fever and work of every kind ground to a sickly halt. Healers tried to stem the tide of death but failed, and indeed, many of them fell sick and died. The accounting of the sick rose every day, and with it grew the number of the dead. The people of the village felt powerless against the plague, they lost all hope. They withered in the face of sickness of the body, and they wilted from diseases of the spirit. They were helpless. They were hopeless. They were forced to face uncertainty alone.

On the ninety-ninth day of the plague, the young man took account of his provisions. What had once been a stockroom filled with vegetables, smoked meats and cheeses, bread, flour, sugar, and salt, now showed only barren shelves. Sacks that had overflowed with beans and rice and apples were slack and empty. Baskets that had once been so full of bread that the young man could barely lift them now held only crumbs. The water jugs were dry and the wine flasks lay hollow—all but one which held a single cup, one last portion, which the young man poured into a cracked and stained clay tankard. He took a careful sip and carried the tankard to his bed chamber. Perhaps the wine would help him sleep soundly, he thought. But no, his worries kept him restless until sunshine filled his window.

The morning sun, oblivious to the pain of the haunted village, rose warm and bright and greeted the young man to his hundredth day of solitude. He left his bed and walked past his pantry once again, and the bareness of his larder chilled him to his bones. It was not merely the anticipation of hunger that caused his dread, nor the terror of the plague. It was the empty baskets and bare shelves, standing as a silent tally of the days he had eaten alone. He could bear the pangs of hunger and even the fear of death—but he was forced now to bear them without companionship or the balm of human kindness.

As if he had been abandoned by the universe and cast adrift.

There was still enough tea in the pantry for one more cup so he went to his kitchen and, as he passed the main door of his home, beside his library and near the stairs, he spied a slip of parchment that had been slid halfway under the door. He picked it up and read:

"The Spirit of Life binds us all together.
No one need be fearful or alone.
The world is our neighbor."

He did not recognize the handwriting and at first he did not understand the message, but the footsteps he heard on his pathway made him open the door just in time to see a man and a woman walking away. They turned towards the young man for the briefest of moments. He did not recognize them, he didn't know their faces. Each one waved to him and smiled. In an instant, they were gone.

Next to his feet, at the threshold of his door, were three large wicker baskets filled with breads and meats and cheeses. Beside them he saw jugs of milk, flasks of wine, and bags of rice and beans. Atop the center basket laid another sheet of parchment. He carried his gifts into his house and unloaded every basket and each bag into his pantry with care. Just this morning the bare shelves spoke to him of hopelessness. Now they spoke of hope. When he had finished his task, he sat at his table with a cup of tea and read the second note.

"We knew that for you today,
this would be the Perfect Gift."

And it was signed "The Voyagers."

The young man sat with the note for a long time, long after his tea had grown cold. That night he cooked a pot of rice and beans and ate it with a slab of cheese and a full tankard of rich wine. After dinner, he sat in the rocking chair in his library reading stories about the Dragon Prince who lives in the Land Beside the Sky and knows the secrets of the Earth and of the stars.

In time, the plague ended, as all plagues do, and the young man left his home to journey through the world. Eventually, he wearied of his travels. He settled at a place beside a stream and a meadow and built himself a house made of fieldstone and cedar. At first he was alone for many days, but then word spread that he had settled there and he became a teacher. The villagers called him the young man, or the wise one. He took for himself the name from the note on the basket of kindness that had changed his loneliness to hope: his Perfect Gift, the gift of knowledge that the Spirit of Life binds us all together. So he called himself The Voyager.

But you, dear Clio, *have known him as Mr. Atros, a traveler who has learned the greatest lesson of all: that the simplest act of kindness can resonate throughout the world, creating goodness, peace, and happiness in the lives of everyone it touches. That was the Perfect Story that the Voyagers of old told me. And that is the lesson of your Perfect Book today.*

What will you do with it? Only time and fate can know.

I'm grateful to you, dear friend, for sharing New Year's Day with me. The Library on Saga Street, The Seven Names of Happiness, and all of the other great books within these walls will always be here when you need them. As for me? Who knows where and when my voyages may take me next? Perhaps one day you will see an old man in a ragged tweed jacket and think of your friend Mr. Atros. Until then, my young friend, consider this.

In all of the countless millennia of creation, you share this specific moment of existence with the people all around you. In order to pierce the isolation that we recognize as unhappiness, and which you called loneliness, you need only open yourself up to the reality that you are a creature of the universe. You are not a solitary traveler on a lonely journey of isolation. You are a sailor on the vast sea of a common humanity, sailing over times and places that will exist only this one time in all eternity.

But this one time is enough—because the possibilities that reside in this slice of eternity are infinite.

Do you think that this sounds too new and strange to be true? It is not. It is not new at all. It is the wisdom of the ages and the music of the spheres. It is found in the secret knowledge of every corner of the world. Plato. Buddha. Confucius. Jesus. The Bible. The Talmud. The Upanishads. They all teach us to connect with the world around us. The sages of all nations have taught the same lessons. Socrates invited the city of Athens to leave their cave of ignorance and experience the sunlight of reality. Moses urged the ancient Hebrews to seek their Promised Land with faith and courage. And Thomas Jefferson made a promise in a New World that men and women could become involved in their society by pursuing happiness.

Experience. Seeking. Pursuit.

Never has a worthy teacher proposed that happiness will come to us while we wait in lethargy and sloth. To the contrary, every great thinker knows that happiness takes effort. It requires your involvement and engagement with the wisdom of the world.

And there is no better, no more successful or righteous way to involve yourself with the community of your fellow humans than with kindness.

Whenever you feel like a spaceship all alone, flying in the void of the dark side of the Moon, remember that what you really are is this: an explorer in a cosmos rich with stars and wonders, connected to futurity and history by the miracle of now.

You are not a stationary molecule of static solitude.

You are not a captive within your own skin, or a prisoner of your own limited identity.

You are—no less than me nor more than any other—an expeditionary traveler through the unlimited opportunities around you.

You are what I have been.

A Voyager.

Travel wisely and with courage for Happiness awaits you.

Your humble guide and eternal friend,
Isaac Hikma

Chapter Eight

GOOD NIGHT TO SAGA STREET

Night had come while Clio read the Voyager's letter.

The snow that had fallen that morning lay glittering on the rooftops and the lawns under the canopy of starlight and the Old Wolf Moon. She had joined the librarian standing at the open door, knowing that her next step would take her away from the amazements of the day.

"Was it everything you hoped it would be?" The librarian asked. "Was it as much as you had hoped for? The book? The day? The stories?"

The young woman's eyes were as wide as saucers as she filled her lungs with winter air.

"Oh yes. It was . . . It is . . . It, it changed me."

"I'm sure it did. It is a book after all, and books change the people who love them. I think that's why Doctor Hikma insisted that his home become a library, a home for books and for the wisdom that lives within them.

"I hope you come back, my dear. *The Seven Names* is one great book but there are many others here and each one of them can change your life. Each one can be the Perfect Gift for you on whatever particular day you open its covers."

She put her hand fondly on Clio's arm. "Good night, Clio. Please pull the door closed when you leave. I must go to meet a very old friend for dinner."

"You're going to meet Doctor Hikma, aren't you? You're going to see him before his next voyage, aren't you?"

The librarian just smiled and pulled her scarf tighter. "I'm glad you decided to come to the library today and I am very glad that I was here to meet you." She looked around at the snow and the stars and then back through the open door at the painting of Doctor Hikma. "It felt good to be back on Saga Street again after so long."

"Back on Saga Street? Again? So long? Old friend?" Clio's voice had dropped to a whisper. "Is your name Sophie?"

The librarian's eyes sparkled. "If you learned anything today I would have thought it would be that people can have many names, just like Happiness."

"But that's not possible unless . . . Unless the Voyager took you with him back to Avalon to meet the Fisher King. Was that what was in your *Read Me* letter along with the deed and the key? Directions to the Moonlight Ship? So that you could drink from the . . .”

But the librarian was no longer listening. She was walking away, the snowfall sparkling all around her. The reflections of the starlight grew dimmer at every step until she vanished in the fog of night and wonder.

All she left behind her was a mystery and the open door.

EPILOG

It has been many years since I was that young woman reading *The Seven Names of Happiness* for the first time. I am now a professor of philosophy at the college where I was once a student. I have a husband, and a son named Isaac. The Perfect Book changed my life as Doctor Hikma knew it would and, since kindness is for sharing, I am sharing it with you.

Sophie was right, *The Seven Names* will be a different book for every reader. It will certainly be different for you than it was for me. You will have your own personal reasons to seek happiness and your Seventh Name may be a different one than mine. I expect that you will have to find it for yourself, but if an old man in a tweed coat ever gives you an envelope marked 'Read This,' don't be surprised. Miracles happen every day. And some of them will happen to you.

I have learned that Hikma is an ancient word for wisdom, and that Isaac was the name of a prophet and a teacher who lived for a very long time and spread knowledge through the world. I like that. The man whom I met as Mr. Atros, and whom the town knew as Doctor Hikma may have had other names in other places too. I imagine him having been a great many other things before, or after, he was a doctor and an occasional librarian.

How many 'Read This' letters has he written, and for whom? Is he writing one for someone else right now? What did Sophie's first letter say? Was it an invitation to Avalon? Was it her Seventh Name?

I hope that I will someday find another book that answers all of these questions.

I still go to the Library on Saga Street and from time to time I read the book again. Sometimes I just sit with the Hikma Collection and reflect on all the ways that men and women can make themselves happy, and all the ways that they so often fail to do that. I always try to be kind and to remember that the greatest wonder of all is the vast world of discovery spread out before us.

Will he ever return?

Will my son meet him on some New Year's Day unfolding?

On one of my visits to the library, I found a book of fairy tales and read one about a girl who left home one morning to take a long walk in a nearby forest where she saw a great many things and learned much about the world. When she returned to her village at dusk, everything was different. Different houses, different streets, different people. She asked everyone what had happened to the old village. They looked at her with confusion and asked her what had happened to the girl who left home that morning to take a walk in the forest. The girl who had learned so much in her wanderings saw a different village. The villagers saw a different girl.

Who was right? Which one had changed?

I hope that *The Seven Names of Happiness* will change the world for you as it has for me. Remember that happiness has many names, and that wisdom can come to us when we least expect it.

I know that this is true.

After all, that is what happened to the girl I used to be.

If you enjoyed
The Seventh Name of Happiness,
read the first chapter of
Dr. Lappas's next book about the power of human fulfillment,

The Philosopher's Third Gift.

Chapter One

Doctor Benjamin Bishop and I had just finished playing chess in his study. We always played chess on Thursday nights. Two games. He always won. On that night though, I almost pulled off an upset in the second game with a Queen's Gambit before he tricked me with a rook sacrifice. "Not bad, Jonah." He always said the same thing after capturing my king. The thought that I might someday win a game kept me coming back Thursday after Thursday.

The glow from the fireplace illuminated the book-lined walls and the horsehair in his antique leather armchairs crunched as we settled back from the board. Everything in that house was old and fine, including the professor. It was almost midnight.

I had been his student in the Brooks University philosophy department for three years as of that night. Doctor Bishop was my dissertation advisor which meant that he decided what I should be researching, when I was finished, whether or not it was any good, and ultimately whether I would ever earn my PhD and the right to be called "Doctor." Advisors controlled their students' academic futures so the relationship was often difficult, even contentious. Not so for us. We shared something much closer to kinship than to discipline.

"I'm going to Paros on Saturday, Jonah," he said, referring to the popular and beautiful Greek island in the Aegean Sea. "My friend Father Dominic made an interesting find there." The professor stood up slowly and walked to his writing desk. He took a key out of his vest pocket and unlocked the middle drawer. When he came back to his chair he handed me a picture frame made out of two squares of glass joined together by tiny screws drilled into each corner. Between the glass there was a small scrap of papyrus. It had rough edges and an irregular shape as if it had been torn from a larger piece. There were a few Greek words on one side but they had faded with time and I couldn't decipher them. I looked at the professor and shrugged.

"*O evthomonia einae tylos*." He took back the frame. "*Evthomonia* is an ancient philosophical term that can mean happiness or human flourishing or fulfillment. *Tylos* means end. But just as in English, that simple word can refer to something more profound. A goal. A reason. A purpose. Or death. 'Happiness is the end.' What do you make of that?"

I had no idea and I couldn't understand what any of this had to do with Doctor Bishop wanting to go to Greece. He saw the confusion on my face.

"So what? Right? Except that *evthomonia* is a word

that comes straight out of Aristotle. Father Dominic borrowed that fragment from the Paros Folklore Museum and sent it to me because he believes that Aristotle wrote the phrase I just read to you. Now that I have seen it, so do I. More than half of Aristotle's writings have disappeared in the centuries since his death: plundered by pirates, destroyed by mold and age, lost beneath the sands of time. Father Dominic and I are both quite positive that this phrase does not appear in any of Aristotle's surviving work. It is a scrap of wisdom that is brand new, but thousands of years old. I believe that when we figure out where it comes from we will have located something truly wonderful."

He considered his next words carefully. "For a long time I have believed that Aristotle wrote a masterpiece about human fulfillment during his old age while he reflected upon everything he had learned throughout his life. If so, it would be the product of a lifetime of brilliance. But no one has ever seen it. At least, not all of it." He tapped the frame which still rested on his lap. "The ramifications of Father Dominic's discovery could be extraordinary. Aristotle was the greatest philosopher of all time; perhaps the wisest person who ever lived. Hearing his ideas about happiness would be a discovery of the most spectacular magnitude."

I remembered that Paros was an island of sailors who often returned home from their voyages with artifacts like maps or scrolls or papyrus which they would sell to souvenir shops and museums. Sometimes they were treasures. Sometimes they were junk. Doctor Bishop was traveling five thousand miles to follow up on a scrap of old writing that might not even mean anything. A quest like that would seem idiotic to most people, but the professor had chased after wilder geese in his life and he had actually caught a few. Maybe he would do it again next week on Paros.

Anyway, Aristotle was the professor's obsession. Even though I mainly studied Plato—he was more fun to read and easier to understand—you couldn't spend any time with Doctor Bishop without picking up some of his enthusiasm for Aristotle. If Doctor Bishop actually did discover something that nobody had ever seen before that would be a very big deal. But it was a very big "if." And there was one more question I had to ask.

"Don't you think you're getting a little old for this kind of adventure, Professor?"

I didn't know Doctor Bishop's exact age, but he was old enough that Brooks carried him on "retired status." He still had an official position but with a reduced workload. He only taught a few courses and he didn't have to advise many doctoral candidates. In fact, he had only one. Me.

"Now Jonah, let's make a deal," he smiled. "When I can no longer beat you at chess or teach you anything new, I'll quit my expeditions. But neither of those things is going to happen in the next two days so I expect I'll be on my way."

"When will you come back?" I wondered.

"That's hard to say. One never knows where the thread of discovery will lead or how long it will take to follow. My return ticket is open and I have an apartment for as long as I need one at Father Dominic's church. It's right across the plaza from the museum. Very convenient."

He looked at the fire and his gaze became very distant, as if he was looking at something a long way—or a long time—away. "Aristotle's teachings about the nature of humanity remain some of the deepest and truest discoveries ever made. If there is something more out there, if there really is a Lost Treatise of Happiness in which Aristotle tells us how to live a life of fulfillment, it could change the world."

"Is that what you expect to find, Doctor Bishop? Something really important?" I wanted a clue.

He considered the final position on the chessboard. "You should never have taken that rook, Jonah." Then he looked back at the fire. "A prize so easy to claim can hide a fearful danger." We spoke for a while about my studies and the dissertation I was supposed to be writing and then Doctor Bishop walked me to the door. The fire was on its last embers. "Read about the Four Causes while I'm gone, Jonah. I have a feeling they could be the key to everything."

The Four Causes? The key to everything? I didn't know what he was talking about but I remember hoping that it wasn't going to turn out to be more Aristotle. He gave me a hug on his front porch and I walked off into the darkness. It was cold and snowy and it took me a long time to walk up the hill to my apartment.

That was twelve years ago. It was the last time I ever laid eyes on Doctor Bishop.

A lot has happened since then.

Watch for Dr. Lappas's third book about
the power of human fulfilment.

The Philosopher's Third Gift

(Projected publication date: Summer 2021)

A brilliant professor seems to have vanished off the face of the earth after embarking on a search for the lost secrets of Aristotle, the greatest philosopher of all time.

While the rest of the world believes him to be dead, two brilliant students receive a series of cryptic letters in which he suggests that he is ready to reveal a monumental discovery of ancient wisdom which has the potential to change the world as we know it and expand the boundaries of human potential.

Can Aristotle's genius reach through the millennia to show the modern world the path to contentment? Is humanity ready to receive the marvelous truths of history's greatest thinker?

Everything depends on the dedication of two young truth-seekers and their ability to decipher the fabulous puzzle of *The Philosopher's Third Gift.*

Readers love

CONQUER LIFE'S FRONTIERS

"No matter how much fame, fortune, or notoriety we attain, we have failed if we're not pursuing our passion and living out our calling and destiny. Spero T. Lappas will take you on a journey of discovery that will lead you to where you are meant to be and who you are meant to become."

Jim Stovall
New York Times bestselling author of *The Ultimate Gift*

"Very well done" and "very rewarding" with "gorgeous phrasing and imagery" and a "beautiful ending."

Writer's Digest 25th Annual Self-Published Book Awards

"*Conquer Life's Frontiers* is a breakthrough book. It will change lives. It walks one through the reasons of how and why we falter. And then it leads one to move forward. It's realistic. It's interesting. It's emotional. It's enjoyable. It's effective. It stands alone in thought-provoking books that can release one from a soul-sucking situation. Bravo to Spero Lappas!"

Patrick Cusick
singer, songwriter, recording artist

"I enjoyed reading *Conquer Life's Frontiers*! It is a memoir, motivational book, and historical analysis all wrapped in one. I especially enjoyed how Dr. Lappas used historical and philosophical tools to illustrate the way people view their past, current, and futures selves. Can anyone jump off the train of unhappiness and follow their dreams? Lappas enthusiastically says *yes* and outlines a course of action that we can take to help us realize our dreams."

Dr. Brian Meier
social psychologist

"Reading *Conquer Lifes Frontiers* feels like having a long conversation with a good friend. It speaks the truth, delivered from a giving heart of a teacher through a tapestry of history, great philosophical minds, superb personal travels and the hard knocks of life. Of the many hundreds of books I have read, this one is surely in my Top Ten. I have read it twice and will surely read it again."

Ronald Calhoon, Esq.
retired attorney, sportsman, world traveler,
listed in *Super Lawyers Magazine*

"Revolutionary life-change almost always requires a catalyst to send us out of our comfort zone and toward the life we envision. *Conquer Life's Frontiers* is that catalyst and Spero T. Lappas is the guide who shows us the way."

Don Hummer, Ph.D.
author; professor, Penn State University

CONQUER LIFE'S FRONTIERS

A Philosophy of Personal Fulfillment

Available NOW

from online booksellers

and your favorite local bookstore.

More information at

https://Alithos.Media

About Spero T. Lappas, PhD

Dr. Spero T. Lappas has studied and written about the philosophy of happiness and personal fulfillment for many years. His breakthrough bestseller, *Conquer Life's Frontiers,* has been praised as "wonderful," "inspirational," "engaging," and "excellent."

He has taught on the faculties of several colleges and universities and has been honored with biographical listings in *Who's Who in the World* and *Who's Who in America,* as well as many other distinguished listings of America's leaders and achievers.

Dr. Lappas graduated with honors from Allegheny College and the Dickinson School of Law, and earned a Doctor of Philosophy degree in American Studies from The Pennsylvania State University. For over forty years he has been one of Pennsylvania's leading trial lawyers. He has written for the *Pennsylvania Magazine of History and Biography, The Champion Magazine, Dickinson Law Review, Harrisburg Patriot-News, N2 Publications, The Encyclopedia of American Studies, Youth Cultures in America, TheBurg*, and other community and academic publications.

In addition to his literary pursuits, he has been an Alden Scholar, a university graduate fellow, a law review editorial board member, a gallery curator, a prize-winning photographer, a world traveler, a tournament Scrabble champion, and a nationally ranked three-weapon fencer.

He is the proud and grateful father and grandfather of a son, a daughter, a son-in-law, a grandson, and a granddaughter to whom he dedicates *The Seventh Name of Happiness*, his second book.

Contact Spero at Spero@SperoLappas.com.

Made in the USA
Middletown, DE
27 October 2020